HOUSE OF TOWER

Rosanna Menck

Table of Contents

CHAPTER ONE

The smell of tangy tomato sauce, melting mozzarella and a tinge of burnt crust wafted over to the two eleven-year-old boys sitting on a couple of boulders at the edge of a clearing. Sky Blue inhaled deeply.

"Pizza has got to be one of my all time favorite foods," he said. He smiled in anticipation, closed his eyes, and tilted his freckled nose skyward for another sniff. He was so absorbed in the pleasure of the moment that he lost his balance and slid off the rock into a heap at the base of Tower Adam's boulder. Tower held his breath until he saw Sky bounce to his feet, slap the dust off his skinny body and hop back onto his boulder.

Tower scoffed. "Ha. You'll eat anything."

"Just 'cause I eat it doesn't mean it's my favorite."

Tower shrugged his shoulders. "I guess not." He watched as his mother approached with two plastic plates of pizza and a couple of cloth napkins. The ancient peasant blouse she wore fluttered in the evening breeze. She had had that blouse as long as Tower could remember. In fact, he was pretty sure he'd seen pictures of her as a teenager in it. Crazy. Tower couldn't believe she still owned something that old, or that it could still be in one piece.

Trivia handed the boys their pizza and drifted away. Tower frowned at his piece.

"I said cheese only, Mom." He plucked off pieces of pineapple and began flinging them to the ground. Sky Blue quickly shoved his plate over to catch them.

"You won't meet your daily minimum," Trivia said.

"I'll have some orange juice. Geez." Sometimes Tower thought his mother carried the good nutrition, healthy living thing a little too far. He bet she had a tablet or a notebook that listed the nutritional content of every morsel Tower and his eight-year-old sister, Teeny, consumed. A tiny smile danced across his face as he pictured his mother poring over a notebook full of protein grams and percentages of vitamin C scribbled in it. And the poor thing would be doing the math by hand, as she didn't even believe in calculators. Geez.

Tower's thoughts were interrupted by the loud slurping sounds Sky Blue was making with his pizza. "Take a breath every now and then, would ya?" Tower said, and bit into his pizza. He stretched the cheese out as far as his arm would go.

Sky Blue finally swallowed and smiled the kind of smile Tower imagined a cat smiled when it swallowed a canary. Although, he hoped cats didn't do that very often in reality.

"You know, you've only got a couple of minutes when the pizza is at its meltiest. After that it's good but it's not at its peak," Sky Blue pronounced.

"You're weird, you know that?"

"Yep. I'm not the one afraid of weird, though. Ready for school tomorrow?"

Tower pulled nervously at a string of cheese. "I think so. I hope so. This year I didn't let my Mom pick out any of my clothes. Middle school has got to be better than grade school."

Tower was an ordinary enough looking kid, medium brown hair and medium brown eyes, average height and weight, but somehow that didn't provide him with immunity from being teased and picked on at school. He couldn't figure it out.

"It's mostly the same old kids though," Sky pointed out.

Tower nodded. That worried him, but there were all those kids from Roosevelt and Carbon River Elementary schools that would be attending Crestview Middle School. They should help Tower slide into anonymity. That was all he wanted—to blend in and not attract any attention. He chomped his pizza and sent silent prayers up to heaven that he would have an easy time of it this year. He hoped that was an okay thing to pray for. To be safe, he sent another silent prayer up that all the kids would have an easy time of it this year. There, that made it so he didn't sound so self-centered.

"Last hot one, then ole Lucifer is shutting down," called Bo, Tower's father. Tower watched as he expertly slid the paddle into the massive brick, wood-burning oven and pulled out a bubbling pizza. He deposited it on the counter where one of the women began to slice it. Like everything in the commune, pizza night was a joint effort. Tower supposed it made life easier for his parents and the other adults to share the work, but living here sure complicated his life.

Tower looked around the clearing surrounding Lucifer. The commune residents sat on old beaten up lawn chairs, fallen logs and boulders. Most were dressed in jeans. Old jeans. And old shirts. In fact, everything here was old and battered.

Which is why Tower did odd jobs over the summer to save up money for new school clothes this year. His family had the notion that buying something new was akin to building a nuclear bomb. Well, that was an exaggeration, but Tower's mother and father sure believed in the whole reduce, reuse, recycle bit to the extreme.

Tower was sick and tired of wearing hand-me-downs from all of the bigger kids in the commune, or wearing garage sale "finds," like the time his mother had found a bunch of brand new surplus t-shirts that were printed with, "1999 Polka-Fest" and bought the whole lot for two dollars. It took all of Tower's imagination, and most of fifth grade, to figure out ways to destroy those t-shirts in a way that didn't look intentional. Ever since, Tower had refused to wear clothes purchased at garage sales. The way he looked at it, garage was only one letter short of garbage, and Tower certainly didn't want to be wearing any-one else's garbage.

But Tower's parents didn't see it that way at all. For them it was all about leaving as little a mark on the planet as possible, and they were appalled at how much good, usable stuff people actually threw out. Tower kind of agreed with them on prin-ciple, but that didn't stop him from wanting some new clothes that fit and looked like the stuff everybody else was wearing.

He was so lost in thought that when Sky plunked a steaming piece of cheese pizza on his plate; it caught him off guard. The pizza slid to the edge of the plate and nearly landed in his lap until Tower hurriedly tipped the plate and slid the pizza back to the middle. Tower cringed at the thought of the burn that would have occurred if the pizza had actually fallen. Sky seemed obliv-ious to the close call.

"Didn't want you to starve," Sky said, as he plopped back on his boulder with his pizza.

"Thanks. And you got it just in time. It's at its meltiest." Tower took a huge, slurpy bite and grinned at Sky, cheese drip-ping down his chin. He was lucky to have a friend like Sky Blue. Maybe this year was going to be okay after all.

A guitar was being tuned. The collection of people gathered in the clearing rearranged their chairs in a haphazard circle, as Bo and Nelson began singing some of the true classics of rock and roll. Occasionally someone would join in and harmonize, but mostly everyone just got comfortable and enjoyed the music.

Tower took a deep breath of the evening air. It was a beau-tiful early September evening, where twilight melts into night without notice. The surrounding air was at that perfect temperature when you felt neither warmth nor chill. Tower stretched his arms out to feel the nothingness better. He turned his arms first up, then down and enjoyed the sensation.

"Dude, is that dancing?" Sky broke the spell. Tower felt his face redden in embarrassment.

"I'm stretching. These boulders can get kind of uncomfortable after awhile, you know?"

"Yeah, right. You were dancing."

"Was not. If I was dancing I'd be moving my feet, not my arms."

"Yeah, and if you were uncomfortable sitting on that rock, you'd be standing up and moving your rear, not your arms," Sky declared.

Tower stood up. "There. Happy?" He stretched exaggeratedly.

Sky hopped off his boulder and shrugged. "Have it your way, dancing boy." He started laughing and running at the same time as Tower charged after him. When Tower was a few feet away, he launched himself at Sky and the two boys tumbled to the ground and began wrestling. Tower got Sky pinned.

"Do you give?" Tower challenged Sky.

Sky shook his head and began singing. "Dancing boy. My name is Tower, but they call me..." He couldn't finish because Tower shifted his weight and Sky Blue could no longer breathe well enough to live, let alone sing. He struggled to push Tower off.

"Offa me. I can't breathe," he huffed, face turning red. Tower bounced on him one final time for good measure, then rolled off. He flopped on his back next to Sky and both boys struggled to catch their breath.

Tower listened to the sounds of the guitar and the singing, then heard the distinct sounds of dishes being gathered up. He hoped his mother couldn't see him lying there in the grass. It was not that he didn't want to do his share of the cleanup, it was more that he didn't want the night to end. Sometimes a moment was so perfect, you wanted to hold onto it as long as possible and make it last. Pizza nights were usually like that. Especially on the last evening before the school year started. After awhile, the guilt got to him and he forced himself to his feet and headed over to where his mother and little sister Teeny were packing up their share of the dishes and silverware.

Since it was too wasteful to use paper plates, the commune residents had purchased a bunch of utensils and dishes from the Goodwill and hauled them back and forth on potluck dinner nights. Sometimes stuff got mixed up, but nobody seemed to care. His mom once said that she'd never be one of those women who marked her name on the bottom of her Tupperware.

"I, mean, honestly," she'd said, "why do people spend thirty dollars on something that can only transport devilled eggs? And then they're so worried they'll lose it, that they can't even enjoy the party. Shoot me where I stand if I ever go around writing my name on things with a Sharpie."

She always said things like, "shoot me where I stand" but Tower still thought it a peculiar thing for a hippie mother to say. And he was rather surprised that she knew what a Sharpie was.

Trivia put the last of their belongings into the tote bag and kissed Bo on the top of his head. "Don't be too long, old man," Trivia said.

"Soon as I got Lucifer tucked in, babe," Bo replied. There were a few dying embers remaining in the pizza oven and Tower knew his father would wait until they were fully extinguished before calling it a night and returning home.

Tower called goodnight to Sky and headed home with his mother and sister. Home was a rather ratty trailer, one of a dozen or so dwellings at the edge of the communal clearing.

There were shacks, motor homes, trailers—you name it. Even an ancient school bus resting on its axle. You could bet that if something was big enough to sleep a person, someone had dragged it out to the commune on some long ago day and set up house in it. And it seemed no one ever thought to do a thing to them since. Tower didn't get it. Didn't anyone but him have eyes? Couldn't they see that everything needed a coat of paint or a can of Rustoleum? He gave up this pointless train of thought and entered the trailer.

He hardly glanced at the bright orange walls and the purple peace signs painted randomly around the living room or the well-worn salvaged furniture as he went down the hall and into his room. If you could call it that.

It was actually only half of a room. There was a cardboard wall Velcroed and duct-taped into place that divided the trailer's second bedroom in two. Cut into the cardboard and folded back, was a door reinforced along the fold with a strip of wood and some antique hinges. Tower supposed he shouldn't complain as he had the half by the window. Poor Teeny had the half by the hall, which meant that Tower had to go through her space every time he entered or left his room. That was one perk of being the oldest.

Tower flopped down onto his stomach on his military style cot and pulled some back-to-school ads from under his pillow. He glanced up at the milk crates on the wall that stored his clothes and sighed. He truly hoped that he had chosen the right clothes for school but it was too late to do anything about it now. He shrugged his shoulders and crumpled up the ads and tossed them into a corner of his room. He laid awake a long time that night.

CHAPTER TWO

The next morning, Tower dressed carefully for school. He was wearing the clothes right out of the J. C. Penney ads. He had studied all the back-to-school ads, and since he was no fashion expert and wasn't exactly surrounded by fashion experts, he decided to buy one outfit from each store. If he didn't fit in this year he'd like to know where the other kids shopped. Mars? Or maybe he could sue the ad guys for misrepresentation or fraud or something. He felt sort of girlie being so obsessed with clothes, but he couldn't help it. He had to fit in this year.

He picked up a hand mirror—the only mirror he had in his room—and angled it this way and that trying to get a good view of himself. It was impossible. Why couldn't they have one decent mirror in the whole house? Even the one in the bathroom wouldn't work. It was all ripply and chipped. Besides, it was way too high to be able to get a full body shot, even if you stood on the toilet. Tower tossed the mirror on his bed and sighed, long and loud. He supposed he looked all right. He knew he looked exactly like the kid in the ad, and that was the best he could do.

He picked up his new backpack and ran his hands over it. This was the best of the best. Top of the line, the salesman called it. The one all the kids were buying. Tower loved it; from the little pouch that could hold a cell phone, to the navy stripe down the middle of the straps. He unzipped it and checked all the school supplies arrayed neatly inside. All set. He hurried out to the kitchen for breakfast.

Tower ducked to avoid the herbs that were dangling from ceiling hooks before they messed up his hair. He slid into his chair just as his mother set down his breakfast. Tower stared at the lumpy oatmeal and scorched toast with dismay.

"I can't eat this." His stomach lurched at the sight.

He watched his sister play with her food. She swirled a puddle of melted brown sugar into patterns with a crust of her toast. Then she made a smiley face with raisins. She raised her spoon and bopped the raisins.

"Every man for himself!" She stirred the oatmeal wildly. "Storm's a coming."

Trivia calmly licked her thumb and used it to wipe a few splashes of brown sugar off Teeny's face, then turned and addressed Tower.

"You can't go off hungry to the first day of school," she said.

Tower looked again at the oatmeal. It was one of the least appetizing things he had ever seen. It didn't even smell edible.

"I'm not hungry."

Teeny crunched her toast into the shape of a shark and plunged it into the oatmeal after the raisins. "Shark! Swim, little people, swim."

Tower hefted his backpack up onto the table and adjusted the straps so it would fit better. Teeny dive-bombed her shark sending oatmeal splashing right onto the backpack. Tower stared at it in horror.

"Teeny! Now look what you've done. I saved up for this all summer." He scooped oatmeal off with a finger, then stuck the backpack in his mouth to suck out the rest of the stain.

Teeny's face fell. "Sorry. I didn't mean to. I was make-believing."

"Wonderful story, Teens. But the storm's cleared. Send your rescue boat mouth out for all your little people. Oh, and in make-believe, it's okay to eat shark," Trivia said.

There was a loud pounding on the door. Tower examined the backpack. It looked completely sucked clean, so he smiled at his sister. "It's okay, Teeny. I got it clean. That's Sky. Gotta go." He dashed for the door batting at a few of the herb bundles in order to get there.

"Careful with the lavender." Trivia closed her eyes and sniffed deeply. "Mmm."

Tower closed the door behind him gratefully, and stared at Sky Blue. He was dressed in totally mismatched clothes that were either a little too big or a little too small. Tower hesitated a second, then kept his opinion to himself.

"Hey."

"Hey." Sky looked up as the door flew open and Trivia shoved something in Tower's hand.

"You can have it to go," Trivia told Tower. He looked down at his hand and saw that his mother had given him a sandwich. A lovely scorched toast and oatmeal sandwich. Tower moaned.

"I don't want to eat this junk any more. I want bacon and eggs like everyone else."

"Funny. You look nice, Sky Blue." She drifted back into the house. Sky beamed at the compliment. Tower snuck another quick look at Sky. Yep, same odd clothes, same weed- whacker hair cut; same Sky. "Mom should get the Polite Lady of the Year award," Tower thought.

"I'll eat it," Sky volunteered. Tower handed him the sandwich and the two boys walked down the long, muddy drive toward a run-down shed. Sky munched on the sandwich with pleasure. Tower shook his head in disbelief. He couldn't think of one thing Sky didn't like to eat. You'd think he'd be as big as a barn door, but he was the skinniest kid Tower knew. Go figure.

Tower opened the shed door, then froze. He had forgotten about the bikes. How could he have done that? Where was his brain? All that planning the perfect outfit would be for nothing if he showed up at school on one of those rusting heaps of metal that barely could be described as a bicycle. He headed out the door.

"I'm walking," Tower said.

"The blue one's not too bad." Sky ran his hand over the blue bike, then tried to disguise the coating of rust that came off in his hand. "Besides it'll take us forever. We'll be late."

"Well then, we're going to have to hurry." Tower turned and started off. Sky waffled a second then hopped on the bike and rode past Tower.

"I'll save you a seat, but you better run part of the way." Sky picked up speed as Tower stared after him. He couldn't believe that Sky would leave without him. He slammed the shed door and hurried off to school.

Great. His best friend had abandoned him and he was probably going to be late. Then everybody would be staring at him. Geez, oh man, oh man. Tower tried to hurry down the street and look nonchalant at the same time.

He slowed down every time he saw somebody—a shopkeeper sweeping the front walk, a delivery person—and gave them one of those "I'm cool" half nods. Being cool was all in the attitude. He had read that some place. Although Tower kind of suspected all the truly cool people never had to fake it. All those Hollywood people must have cool running all through them, like blood or plasma or something.

The school loomed in front of him. It looked huge and confusing and Tower wished for a second that he could turn right around and go somewhere, anywhere, else. Maybe they could use an eleven-year-old kid in the circus. Or he could join one of those fishing boat crews in Alaska, like he saw on the Discovery

Channel in science class. Neither of those things sounded anywhere near as scary as going in that school. He stood there fro-
zen for a few more minutes then decided that as he had no other
choice but to go in, he would be far better off to do it before the
bell rang, not after.

CHAPTER THREE

Tower opened the classroom door and tried not to look out of breath as he scanned the room for Sky Blue. There he was, waving his hand, as noticeable as if he had hung a neon sign. Luckily no one was paying attention so Tower walked as casually as he could and slid into the chair that Sky had saved for him. He'd made it just in the nick of time. Whew. He took his backpack off and surreptitiously checked out the other students. The good thing was they also looked straight out of the Sunday ads. Tower's mood lightened. He was beginning to think this had a shot at being a good year.

Tower heard a loud throat clearing from the teacher standing at the front of the classroom. She was kind of pretty with long brown hair tied up in a pony tail, and mid-adultish in age. Not almost collegey and not anywhere near parenty, Tower assessed.

"Good morning, everyone. My name is Mrs. Jones and I'll be your home room and world geography teacher for this year. First off, everyone shut off any pagers or cell phones, then I'll call roll."

The majority of the class started scrambling around into their backpacks and pockets to shut off their various electronic devices. Of course the nifty little pouch on Tower's awesome new backpack hadn't so much as a gum wrapper in it, let alone a cell phone. Tower knew that, and Sky Blue knew that, but Tower was bound and determined that no one else would know that, so he pulled up the Velcro flap and faked shutting something off. Sky Blue caught Tower's eye and started to open his mouth, but snapped it shut when he caught the glare that Tower sent penetrating through his eyes and into the tingly part of Sky's brain.

Mrs. Jones picked up a sheet of paper and began calling roll.

"All right, let's get started," she said as she glanced at her roster, hesitated a second, then called, "Uh, Adam Tower."

There were a few snickers scattered around the classroom, and Tower fidgeted in embarrassment but remained silent. Mrs. Jones looked up quizzically.

"It's Tower Adam, ma'am. His Dad wanted to name him Howard..." Sky Blue's voice trailed off. Tower tried to shush him, but Sky ignored him. In the back of the classroom, Jeremy, a kid who looked like a linebacker in training, poked a couple of his friends and made a peace sign. They all started laughing. The teacher glared at them and waved her hand for Sky to continue.

"...but his Mom was pretty out of it and thought he said Tower," Sky said.

Jeremy rolled his eyes and acted woozy. Mrs. Jones didn't notice, but Tower did. He remembered Jeremy from last year, although he must have done some super-sized eating over the summer. He had moved into the area shortly before the end of fifth grade, and had hooked up with Matt and D.J. and the three had created their own little bullying gang, dumping kids in garbage cans and swirling their heads in toilets. And that was back when Jeremy was an average sized kid.

"I see. So is Tower present?" Mrs. Jones asked.

Tower raised his hand and prayed she would hurry up and not ask anything else. The last thing he needed was to attract the attention of those goons in the back. Why couldn't he have been named Andy or Dan or even Jonah? Tower. Geez. Even though he sometimes liked his name, he had to admit it sounded very hippieish. He turned and scowled at Sky Blue.

"I'm gonna kill you," he whispered.

"What? Why? What'd I do?" Tower continued to scowl until Sky dropped his head and mumbled a pathetic little sorry. Tower forgave him right off the bat, 'cause after all he was his best friend, and it wasn't like he had said anything that wasn't true. Tower turned his eyes back to the teacher and faked an interest in the rest of roll call.

Somehow Tower got through the rest of the day without incident. He trotted down the steps of the school, glad to be out in the late afternoon sunshine. He walked Sky over to the bike racks and said goodbye, then began the walk home, at a more leisurely pace than the one he'd taken in the morning.

He was about halfway home when he heard the first taunts. He knew even without turning to look that it was Jeremy, Matt and D.J. Who else could it be?

"Hurrying back to your little commune? How's that work, exactly? Do you all live in a big tent? Do you even have running water?" Jeremy asked.

Tower forced himself to ignore the insults and keep walking.

"Oh, Howard, where's your little friend? What is it? Cloud Nine?" Jeremy asked. The boys roared with laughter.

"No. That's not it. Uhh. Sunny Rainbow? Nah, I remember now. Sky Blue. Yeah, where is the other hippie freak?" Jeremy continued.

Tower was not going to give Jeremy the satisfaction of responding. Answering back was only going to egg him on. He kept his eyes glued straight ahead and put one foot in front of the other. He had to force himself to keep the same pace even though he felt like running. You had to treat these guys the same way you would if you came upon a pack of stray dogs, or hyenas, or jackals, or... Tower was forced to break off his scary animal train of thought when Jeremy gave him a shove.

"Knock it off," Tower said in as calm a voice as he could muster. Jeremy started dancing around in front of him, in back of him, and to the side of him blocking Tower in every direction until he was forced to stop. Jeremy flicked him on the head with his middle finger. Tower was insulted and more than a little scared. Jeremy looked huge up close. Tower drew his shoulders up, puffed out his chest, and tried his best to look fierce even though his heart was pounding in his chest so hard he could hear his pulse by his ears.

"Cut it out," Tower demanded in a voice that he was quite pleased wasn't quavery and wimpy sounding.

"Or what? Whadda ya gonna do, hippie boy? Flip me a peace sign?" Jeremy asked.

The boys were so engrossed in their confrontation that none of them noticed they were being observed by a middle-aged woman sitting on her porch a short distance away. She sipped from a cup and watched with interest.

"Come on, kid," she said under her breath. "Give him a taste of his own medicine."

Tower stoically tried to step around Jeremy but he was like one of those annoying flies that dive bomb your ears right when you're trying to fall asleep. He dodged left, then right, then behind and before Tower could avoid it, Jeremy yanked on Tower's backpack so hard that the strap ripped. Instinct took over and Tower furiously swung the other strap off his shoulder and sent the backpack whirling hard through the air straight for Jeremy's head. Jeremy had no time to react. The heavy backpack was going to knock him somewhere into the next county. That is, until Tower jerked it back moments before impact. The boys stared at each other.

"Smart move, granola boy. That thing woulda hit me, you woulda been toast," Jeremy said. He stared down Tower for a few more seconds, then nodded at his friends and they all headed down the block.

Tower watched them go. The adrenaline that had his heart thumping so hard a few minutes ago was draining away, leaving him with this weird noodly leg thing. He wasn't at all sure that he could walk.

"You have amazing self restraint. That kid deserved a big wallop."

Tower almost jumped out of his brand new Nikes. Well, that proved his legs still worked, but this day was playing havoc with his heart rate. He looked at the woman speaking to him. She was somewhere around his father's age, with short dark hair and glasses. She was wearing old jeans, and a lightweight tan sweater.

"Yeah, he did but that's not how I was brought up." Tower looked sadly at his backpack.

"I wish he had hit me instead of ripping my backpack. I barely got to use it." Tower sighed loudly. The woman patted him on the shoulder and reached out for the backpack. She examined it closely.

"Ah, that's easy to fix. I could sew it for you."

Tower was torn with indecision. It's not like his mother couldn't sew; it was how she would sew it that worried Tower. She would probably use pink thread or sew a little heart or something equally hideous in the name of creativity. On the other hand, he didn't know this woman from Adam and according to all the beware-of-strangers lectures he'd gotten through the years, shouldn't trust her.

The woman must have sensed Tower's unease because she smiled gently and introduced herself.

"I'm Rosemary." She held out the backpack. "Well?"

"Uh, I'm Tower. You really think you can fix this?"

"Piece of cake."

Tower looked at Rosemary. She certainly didn't look like the kind of big bad stranger everyone warned you about. And didn't his Dad always say, "trust your judgment," when Tower asked him for advice? Well it was time he put his father's advice to the test.

"Matching thread?"

Rosemary nodded. "Matching thread."

That was enough for Tower. He followed her up the steps.

CHAPTER FOUR

Tower looked around Rosemary's house curiously. It was decorated in monochromatic tan colors with comfortable looking furniture. There were black and white photographs of buildings hanging on the walls and absolutely no clutter.

"Wow." Tower couldn't help himself. "I mean, this is nice."

"Thanks. Wait here. I'll go get a needle."

Tower stretched his arms up and gazed at his hands in amazement. He didn't know it could feel so good to not have dried herbs bumping up against them. He sighed, one of those sighs that say, "I'm in heaven," and twirled around in pure joy.

"Ahem." Rosemary cleared her throat and Tower jumped back into a normal posture, totally embarrassed. Great. The woman hadn't even known him for five minutes and here he was dancing around her living room like some kind of prissy ballerina. He wished the floor would swallow him up but Rosemary didn't seem to pay much attention. She simply sat in a chair, put on a pair of reading glasses and began to thread a needle.

"Go ahead, kid. Sometimes a body has a need to twirl. I understand."

"No. I'm all right now, honest." Tower took a deep breath and decided tell her. "It's your place. It's so...nothing hangy-downy. I can move. I guess what I'm trying to say is; I like it," he finished in a rush.

"It suits me. Almost finished. Don't want to make you too late; your mother will worry."

Tower started wandering around. He peered into a doorway and saw an orderly kitchen.

"Nah. She doesn't know what time school gets out. My friend and I always chill for awhile at the start of the school year so we have an hour or so of free time the rest of the year."

Tower stood in front of a bookcase and perused the titles.

"What do you do with all this stolen free time?"

"Mostly eat contraband food." Tower fiddled with a few of the books.

"Contraband food?"

"Yeah, you know hamburgers and hot dogs and stuff."

Rosemary smiled. "I would have guessed candy and dough-nuts." She bit off the thread and examined her work. She seemed pleased.

Tower shook his head. "Oh, those are only on the restricted list." He hoped that was the end of the questions. He didn't feel like going into all the weirdness that was his life. It was hard explaining something that Tower himself sometimes didn't understand. He turned away from the bookcase and accidentally bumped a folder from the bottom shelf. It spilled a few pieces of paper out. Tower bent over to pick them up.

The picture of a house under construction on one of the brochures caught Tower's eye. The title read, "Neighbors For Neighbors." He opened it and read the information inside.

"What's this?" he asked Rosemary.

She glanced up. "It's an organization I volunteer with. People of all ages and walks of life come together and build a house from the ground up, and before you know it another deserving family has a new place to call home. It's amazing."

"You mean you build houses and give them away to poor people?" Tower was intrigued, but suspected this was too good to be true.

"Well, if they qualify." Rosemary handed over the backpack. "How's that look?"

Tower held up the backpack and checked it out. He couldn't tell that there had ever been a rip. The thread matched perfectly. He gave an experimental tug on it to test for strength. The repair held.

"This is great. Thanks. So...this house thing is only for poor people?" He couldn't help himself. He was starting to get one of those itchy, coming up with an idea feelings. Maybe he'd been going about this all the wrong way. Maybe new clothes weren't enough. After all, even if he had the best clothes in the world, he still went home to a commune. And that was always going to give guys like Jeremy major ammunition. But if he lived in a house, well, that was as normal as it got, right? Tower entertained this idea a little longer.

"Low income, disabled, you know, people who need a little help. There's a website you can check out if you're interested," she said.

Tower was afraid he sounded too eager so he tried to keep a neutral look on his face. It also occurred to him that he should be going, as the backpack was finished. He tried to think of an excuse to dawdle because he liked it here. He liked being able to move freely, he liked the lack of clutter, but he especially liked the neutral tan color on the walls, which felt as soothing to his eyes as snuggling into a soft blanket did to his face.

"Well, thanks for fixing this. I appreciate it." Tower reluctantly opened the front door, which gave off a loud squeak. He swung it back and forth. "I could maybe come back and fix this for you; that would be fair." He looked up hopefully.

Rosemary smiled. "I'd like that."

Tower hopped off the front porch steps. He was in a good mood. Even though Jeremy had tormented him and ripped his brand new backpack, he felt like skipping. Of course, he didn't do that, but he did take a joyful little hop every now and then.

CHAPTER FIVE

Tower turned up the gravel driveway toward home. Pink Floyd was blaring out of speakers in the shed. That meant Bo was home. Although all of the adults at the commune listened to the classic rock of the sixties and seventies, the shed was Bo's workshop and if he was in there you could be sure that the music would be on. Tower suspected Bo had unfulfilled dreams to be a rock star, but his father claimed that he was merely a connoisseur of good music. As Tower drew closer to the shed he saw Sky Blue pumping a flat tire on the blue bike.

"Told you they were all junk," Tower said.

Sky Blue looked up. "It's just a tire. Besides, I still beat you home."

"Yeah, thanks to you I nearly got killed today. Jeremy wanted to fight."

"How's that my fault? Besides, you look okay to me," Sky Blue answered.

"I said Jeremy wanted to fight. I didn't say I actually did fight. I walked away," Tower said.

Bo appeared from around the side of the shed and clapped Tower on the shoulder. "I'm proud of you, son. Remember it's the strong man who walks away," he said.

"I should have knocked his nose back into his brain, if he even has a brain." The minute Tower said this he regretted it. Not because he felt bad saying Jeremy was brainless. No, that part he didn't regret at all. It was the nose knocking part that he was going to pay for with one of his father's lectures. Tower hoped it would be a short one but was a little worried when Bo sighed long and sorrowfully.

"Tower. That kind of wrong thinking's what messes this world up. We need your generation to be visionaries for peaceful solutions to problems. Wars are being fought right now because men didn't learn this when they were young."

Tower hurried to say something that would keep the rest of the lecture from happening. "I know nothing good comes of fighting. Sorry, sometimes I say stupid things." He looked up and saw the relief in his father's eyes. Whew. That was close.

Tower was glad he had managed to dodge a true fight even though Jeremy had done his best to provoke him. Tower had ignored the pushing and the name-calling. He'd even ignored the totally insulting head thumping. And it took all his will power not to haul off and slug the nasty bully when he ripped his backpack. Which would have been for nothing anyway, since Rosemary had sewn it up good as new.

"You're a good kid, ya know that?" Bo asked.

"Thanks." Tower felt a warm glow in his center.

But then Sky Blue had to add his two cents worth and turn Tower's warm glow into molten lava. "You would have avoided the trouble entirely if you had ridden a bike like me."

"I didn't want to ride one of those crummy bikes, okay? Not today, not tomorrow; not ever! And if you were a true best friend you would know that and you wouldn't have left me to walk by myself." The words seemed to burst out of him of their own free will. Tower was shocked at himself and felt awfully crummy when he saw the hurt look on Sky's face. Which, in a way, made him even madder.

Bo shook his head. "Go change into your work clothes, son, then come scrub bricks."

Tower stomped off, kicking at mud clumps as he went. Geez, what a crazy day. One minute he felt good and the next, incredibly grouchy.

Tower stormed into his room and was halfway out of his pants when Teeny wandered in. Tower quickly yanked his pants back up.

"Get out of my room! I'm trying to get dressed, here," he hollered.

"You should have locked it," she said calmly.

"I forgot. So scram." Tower pointed to the door, but Teeny ignored him and crouched down by the bed.

"I'm hiding from Mom. She wants to give me Icky Nation. I barely even sniffed. I thought we lived in one nation under God. Why does it have to be so icky?"

Tower tried to reassure Teeny. "It's echinacea, Teeny, not icky nation. Be glad it's not garlic and orange juice. That sweats out of your pores for days and no one can stand to get next to you. Anyway, you can't hide for long. If we had a real house..." Tower gazed off into space, dreamy-eyed, then jerked back to the present. "Besides, you won't die. It just feels like it for a few minutes. Then Mom will give you some cranberry juice. You better go."

Teeny began to wail and act out one of her stories.

"The wicked stepmother is about to drip poison down the fair maiden's throat, when up rides the King to save her." She melodramatically grabbed at her neck.

"Fair maiden," Tower played along, "no king is more powerful than our mother. Go take your medicine like a brave knight."

"But I'm a girl," she protested.

"Don't you know? Girls are some of the bravest knights around," Tower said. With that, Teeny smiled at him, straightened her posture bravely, and left.

Little sisters. Tower shook his head and made sure he securely latched the door with its special Velcro latch system, and hurried to change his clothes so he could scrub bricks. His father had already given him that, 'I'm disappointed in you' look after Tower hollered at Sky. Tower sure didn't want him to think he was shirking his chores.

In the kitchen, Teeny was carrying on with her fairy tale. She held a three-foot length of bamboo out in front of her like a knight's sword and held it high over her head.

"I, noble knight lady Christina, will take thy poison from the wicked stepmother so my fair kingdom shallest be spared." Teeny bowed graciously then lifted her face to accept her poison.

Trivia joined in the spirit of the game, grabbed a dish towel and flung it over her head. She walked with a wicked limp toward Teeny with her potion of echinacea.

"I promise to spare the kingdom if you willest just swig my poison verily," she cackled. She ceremoniously filled a dropper full of foul brown fluid and squirt it down Teeny's brave little mouth. Teeny spluttered but swallowed then hopped around the room gagging.

Trivia whipped off the dish towel and switched roles, becoming the rescuer. She quickly poured a glass of cranberry juice and proffered it to Teeny.

"Noble knight lady. You have saved us all. Let me revive you with my mead," Trivia said.

Teeny grabbed the glass and chugged a few swallows. "Mead? I should get a Coke or something after that, Mom."

Tower dashed by his mother and sister on his way out the door. Teeny seemed to have recovered from her echinacea ordeal. Tower couldn't blame her for her theatrics. Echinacea tasted nasty and burned a hole wherever it touched and even if it made his colds shorter, Tower would just as soon cough and sniff for a little longer, if he could avoid having to swallow the disgusting potion.

CHAPTER SIX

Tower joined his father and Sky Blue where they sat next to the shed, scrubbing the mortar off of old bricks with putty knives, wire brushes and buckets of water. They worked in companionable silence for awhile. That is, no one was talking, but the classic rock music that pulsed forth from the shed set the rhythm for their work.

Tower found himself speculating about living in a normal house. One like Rosemary's. Before today he had never thought about living anywhere besides their sustainable community.

Sustainable community! Ha! That was just the twenty-first century description for a commune. It still meant that a group of people with similar views on the world and environment lived together on a jointly owned piece of land, and tried to be as self sufficient as possible and not rely on government services. They grew their own food, had their own well for water, and generated much of their energy with solar panels and a windmill. Everyone did their share of the work around the community and most of the adults also worked at a variety of jobs in town.

Tower had always known that the rest of the world didn't live like this. Now, however, he saw how truly weird it was. There was no way the kids at school were ever going to treat him as normal while he lived out here. He began to fantasize about a real house. What a fool he was to think that a cool backpack and trendy clothes would make a difference in how the other kids treated him this year. He needed a house. He wasn't greedy. He didn't need a fancy mansion. A simple ordinary house like the kind Rosemary lived in would work fine.

He realized his mother would still need to dry herbs for her business, but he figured in a house there would bound to be enough rooms so the herbs didn't have to be in the main living areas where he would run into them all the time. And, he thought, dreamily, he could have his own room. Not a half of a room. A whole room with a regular door and a closet, and made out of wood, not cardboard. The idea of this house kept teasing at his brain. He snuck a look over at his father.

"Dad," he asked, ever so casually, "how poor are we?" Tower held his breath anxiously, although he was not exactly sure what he needed the answer to be.

His father looked up, startled. "Not poor at all, son."

Tower shook his head impatiently. "Yeah, yeah. We've got each other and our health and all that. But, you know on our tax return stuff. Does it seem like we're poor?" He focused on the bricks, and acted nonchalant, scrubbing furiously. His father took such a long time answering that Tower began to grow nervous. Finally, unable to stand it any longer he looked up.

"Dad. You do file tax returns, don't you?" Tower asked.

"Of course I do. It's just, on paper, our finances look a little lean."

Tower bowed his head so his father wouldn't see how this information pleased him. He dared to get his hopes up.

"But don't you worry none. We got plenty. A lot of my business is done on the barter system. A straight trade don't fit neatly into the government's 'wages, tips and other compensation' way of thinking," Bo said.

Tower was afraid his father might start asking questions so he tried to distract him by throwing his brick onto the growing pile of clean bricks. "You going to add on to Lucifer?"

"Nah. Mrs. Holt down on Maple wants me to build her a path," Bo said.

"She probably wants you to use new bricks," Tower said.

Bo lifted up a brick and examined it. "Nothing wrong with this here brick. Got a lot of use left in it."

Tower was unconvinced. "People like new."

"We know better though, don't we? I, for one, thank you Bo for saving this planet for the next generation. That's us, Tower," Sky said.

Tower could have done without the commentary from his best friend. "Sky. Sometimes you tick me off. I'm trying to have a conversation here with my old man, and you go kissing up to him."

Sky Blue was offended. "I'm not kissing up. I'm serious."

"Well knock it off."

"Tower, son, what's going on?" Bo asked.

"Nothing. Hey, do you think we have enough bricks to build a house? I'm kidding."

Tower could have kicked himself for that last question. His father was looking at him strangely, and Tower had lived long enough to know if parents start looking at you strangely, it's bad news. Sometimes you don't know what you've said or done to get the look, other times, like now, you know exactly what you've done. Either way, Tower would rather never see 'the look.'

"Tower. Is there something you want to share with me?"

Tower shook his head. "No. I'm fine." He knew his father was still looking at him, but he pretended to be absorbed in the task of brick washing, and didn't look up. After awhile, Tower snuck a peek up and saw that Bo had gone back to work also. Whew. That was close.

Bo might not have been looking at Tower, but Sky sure was. He gave Tower a quizzical look, and Tower gave him back a look that said, "I'll tell you later." It was great how Tower and Sky knew each other so well that they could communicate without speaking. Although, Tower suspected that Sky ignored half of the messages that Tower sent with his face. Maybe Tower should check his facial expressions in the bathroom's old, ripply mirror and see if they looked right. It could be that he needed practice. Tower practiced making a few faces right now but hurriedly stopped when he felt Bo staring at him once again.

"Whoa. I thought I felt a sneeze coming on. Don't you hate it when the sneeze gets stuck?" He rubbed his nose vigorously, then to change the subject, Tower tossed the last brick on the pile. "All finished. Sky and I have some homework to get to, is that okay?"

He held his breath, while his father looked at him intently. Tower pasted the most innocent look he had in his facial expression repertoire and looked back at Bo. He felt his face tingle and his eyes started to water, but finally his father nodded.

"Sure. Thanks for the help, boys," Bo said.

Tower jumped to his feet and grabbed Sky's arm. They headed back to the trailer the gravel crunching beneath their feet. Tower ignored the look Sky was giving him until they were safely inside Tower's room.

"Okay, I'm about to bust. What is going on with you?" Sky asked.

Tower flopped on his stomach and reached under his cot for his backpack, then pulled out the brochure that he'd gotten from Rosemary. He tossed it to Sky.

"I think I feel a plan coming on," he said.

Sky Blue flipped through the brochure and groaned. "I don't know if I can survive one of your plans."

"It's nothing dangerous," Tower said.

"Okay. I give. What's up?" Sky asked.

Tower thought about teasing Sky and making him wait a little longer, but he couldn't be that mean.

"I'm going to get me one of these houses." Wow. He didn't realize how ridiculous it sounded until he said it out loud. If it sounded crazy to him and it was his idea, Tower could imagine how it would sound to other people. Not that he was going to tell anyone but Sky—at least for now.

"What?" Sky asked. "How are you going to do that?"

Good question. Maybe Tower shouldn't have even told Sky about this until he had had a chance to think it all the way through. But he did what he usually did, which was to blurt something out as soon as he thought it. Tower shook his head in disgust. He needed to work on that.

"Well. I haven't figured it all out yet. I have to go to the library and check out their web site, then I'll come up with my plan. I think I can do most of the application online." Tower gazed off into space. "Think about it. If I lived in a house those jerks would have nothing to pick on me about."

"What do your parents think about it?" Sky took one look at Tower's face. "Don't tell me. You aren't going to tell them, are you?"

Tower shook his head. "Not yet. I've barely looked into this."

"Oh. Would they build the house out here?" Sky's usually cheerful face was subdued.

"Are you crazy? If they did that it wouldn't change anything. I would still be the weird kid who lived on a commune," Tower said.

Sky remained silent. Tower finally sensed something was wrong and looked up from the brochure. Sky looked bummed out. Tower hurried to reassure him.

"Don't worry. You can come over any time. Hey, maybe we can get you a house too," Tower said. Tower smiled broadly. He thought that was a fine idea.

Maybe they could still be next door neighbors. They could mow their lawns on Saturday mornings together. Tower had never mown a lawn before, but he thought it looked like fun. He would have to figure out a way to get his father to buy a lawn mower with an engine, though. It would be just like him to buy one of the little twirly-bladed ones that you see in movies from the nineteen fifties. He added that to the mental list he was compiling. It looked like there was going to be a whole lot Tower was going to have to figure out if he was going to put this plan in action and actually have it work out.

Tower broke out of his little daydream when he realized that Sky hadn't said anything in awhile. He looked up. Sky did not look very happy.

"Hey. Don't look like that. This is my one chance to have a house. And a house means you're normal." Tower looked around his little space and started to daydream. "My own room. Wood floors and real curtains, not like those." He stared disgustedly at the macramé window shades, then rummaged under his pillow and pulled out some sample paint cards and tossed them at Sky Blue.

"I almost forgot. What color do you like?"

Sky glanced at them dubiously. "They're all brown."

"No. That's sandstone. And that's earthen glow..."

"Brown." Sky interrupted emphatically.

"You're not much help." Tower turned away and thumbtacked them to his cardboard wall.

"You don't get it, do you?" Sky shook his head in disgust and stormed out.

Tower felt a twinge of remorse at upsetting Sky. He didn't waste much time worrying about it though, because Sky was an easygoing guy who didn't let things bother him for long. Tower knew that things would be back to normal tomorrow.

He lay back on his cot and stared at the color samples he had gotten on his way home from Rosemary's. The lady at the paint store had told him that the neutral colors were the way to go. They were fashionable and matched any design style. Tower doubted that he had a design style, but he liked the idea of being able to match it to his wall paint once he figured out what it was. He sighed. This project was the biggest thing he had ever taken on in his whole entire life. It made him tired to even think about.

After a few more minutes of wishful thinking and day-dreaming, Tower pulled out several sheets of notebook paper and began making a list. He had a feeling the list was going to be too long to keep track of by memory.

CHAPTER SEVEN

The kitchen was in more of a state of chaos than usual. There were boxes and little bottles and medicine droppers everywhere. A stack of hand-drawn labels sat on a corner of the kitchen counter.

It was bottling time for Trivia's home-brewed echinacea, and Bo and Trivia were working with an easy camaraderie that said they had done this countless times before. The echinacea came from an organic herbal supplier in a ground form that sort of resembled ash from a fireplace. In order to steep out the antimicrobial properties of the herb and to preserve it, Trivia put it into vodka and let it sit for at least six months. Now that it was ready, they poured the tincture from the vodka bottles through a funnel into the small medicine bottles. They would be offered for sale at the commune's roadside stand.

It was one of their most successful products. People were eager to strengthen their immune systems to stay healthy and avoid having to take commercial medicines with all the side effects that came with them. There was a little bit of a controversy a few years ago, when the authorities discovered that the tincture contained alcohol. The liquor control board sent out inspectors who were prepared to shut Trivia's business down. When they saw how tiny the bottles were, and that the dosage was a mere dropper full, they gave Trivia a special license to sell them. The packaging had to be labeled correctly, and she couldn't claim that her tincture prevented or cured any illnesses, as that violated Food and Drug Administration rules.

Trivia was happy to go along with those conditions and every year she sold out.

Bo wiped down the bottles with a clean cloth, then carefully capped them. "Good batch this year?" he asked.

Trivia nodded, pleased with her product. "Yeah, strong. Half the batch is already presold and these will fly off the shelves, with all that bird flu scare going on."

"Yeah, I understand that. I'm scared of bird flu. And flesh eating bacteria and all the rest of those weird microbes out there waiting to make a feast of me." Bo was only partly joking. Trivia poked him.

"Your immune system should be as strong as a horse with all the good vegetables and herbs I feed you," she replied. "If those bugs get anywhere near you, they'll get such a thumping, that they'll jump ship to the poor vulnerable sap standing next to you who makes the mistake of shoving all those Big Macs and fries into his body."

Bo reached over and gave her a squeeze. "You're right. I have nothing to worry about. You take such good care of us, sweetie. By the way, Tower seem okay to you?"

Trivia filled the last of the bottles and handed it to Bo to cap. "Yeah. Teeny has a little cold, though. Want a squirt?"

"Couldn't hurt. But I meant...Tower acting weird lately?" Bo tried to keep the tone light.

"A little picky with food, maybe. Why?"

Trivia readied a dropper full of echinacea and held it over Bo's mouth. He opened his mouth and Trivia squirt the liquid into the little pocket under his tongue. He held it there a few seconds, then shivered as he swallowed it down. He pulled Trivia into his arms and gave her a damp smooch. "Love that burn, woman."

He got back to the subject of Tower. "Anyway. Tower was asking me about a house. I think maybe he's outgrown that little room."

"Oh, that. Teeny wandered into his room when he was changing. I think he was a little embarrassed. I'll have a talk with her," she said.

"I suppose that could be the reason. Are these bottles ready for the labels?"

They began slapping the decorative labels on the little bottles and packed them into the various sizes of recycled cardboard boxes.

Bo's thoughts drifted. He looked around the trailer's kitchen and living room. He loved the wild colors and the jumble of items everywhere. It felt energetic and life giving. It was crowded, but most of the belongings were hand crafted by Trivia, which made Bo feel connected to them. He was troubled to think that Tower might not feel the same way. He supposed it could be a privacy thing. Trivia was right. No eleven-year-old boy wanted his little sister to walk in on him when he was changing his pants. Still, Bo decided to think on it some.

As soon as he and Trivia were done with the packaging of the echinacea, Bo pulled out his trusty old guitar. He ran his hand on it lovingly and flexed his fingers. He sat down on the threadbare couch and strummed a few chords. He always had his best ideas when his brain was freed up of forced thinking and just allowed to cruise along with the music.

CHAPTER EIGHT

The next day Tower went to all kinds of trouble to avoid running into Jeremy and his friends. He figured the less they saw of him the less it would cross their minds to torment him. In the morning, he circled the building and entered the door by the gym and walked as slowly as he could toward his class. He waited until practically the last minute before the bell, then rushed into the classroom.

Tower slid into his seat. He began to feel a tingling sensation on the back of his neck, the kind you get when someone is staring at you. Or maybe three someones. He felt an almost uncontrollable urge to turn around, even though he knew that would be the worst thing he could do. It would be like egging the bullies on. He forced himself to keep his eyes forward, staring at the map of the world hanging on a bulletin board so hard that his eyes started to water. At this rate, he wouldn't even have to study. Tower would know all those countries by heart. What a stinky way to do well in school.

What made someone become a bully, anyway? Maybe they were dropped on their heads at birth, or bitten by rabid dogs. There was nothing else that explained why kids could like being so mean. The few times in his life that Tower had done something mean, he had felt so bad about it that he apologized for about an hour, and then felt bad every time he remembered it. Kids like Jeremy and Matt and D.J. must not have a conscience that worked the same way that Tower's did, or they would not be getting much sleep at night.

At lunchtime, Tower slunk into the cafeteria and tried to scope out where the bully boys were sitting. He kept having to dodge behind one tall kid after another, and peek around them until he finally spotted the troublemakers. Tower skirted around the perimeter of the cafeteria and found a table behind a post. The table was only partially hidden, but it was out of the direct line of sight of Jeremy's table. Short of being beamed up to Mars, which Tower thought was a great idea, this table was going to have to do. He sunk down onto the bench in relief, and then almost shot into orbit when Sky plopped down next to him.

"Don't do that. You scared me to death! How did you even find me?" Tower asked.

"Came in that door. Saw you right off." Sky pointed to a door a little behind and to the side of their table. Tower rolled his eyes in disbelief.

"Great." At least he was safe for now, since he knew exactly where the bullies were, so he may as well eat his lunch, but tomorrow was another story. Tower looked in his lunch sack and sighed. He was going to have to add packing his own lunch to his list of 'How to be Normal.' It was getting to be a very long list.

"Whatcha got?" Sky asked as he pulled out his sandwich.

Tower carefully pulled out his main dish and sat it out on the table for Sky to see for himself. A half of an avocado was cut side down on a little plate. The back of the avocado was studded with roasted pumpkin seeds and sliced almonds in rows on the fat, round part of the avocado. The skinny end had small pieces of black olives pushed into it to make a face.

"I've got a porcupine," Tower replied.

Sky looked at the creation and nodded his approval. "Cool. Your mom sure can come up with some crazy lunches."

"Crazy is right." Tower pulled out a trio of tangerines and Japanese rice crackers to round out his meal. "She gave me a knife but no fork, so I think I'm supposed to put a little avocado on the crackers."

"That makes sense. Can I have one of the tangerines? You have three."

Tower rolled a tangerine across the table to Sky.

"Sure. They're pretty good. Sweet and no pesky seeds."

"Yeah, I hate that. You lose most of the juice trying to spit the seeds out. So, have you come up with any more plans?"

"The plan I'm working on is big enough. What do you mean, any more plans?" Tower answered. He smoothed out the foil that had wrapped his avocado, folded it neatly and returned it to his lunch sack. He took a bite of porcupine cracker.

"I hate this plan. I don't want you to move." Sky peeled the tangerine effortlessly and shoved little slices into his mouth.

"Come on, Sky. You're my best friend. I'm counting on you to be on my side. Besides, even if I can figure everything out, it's going to take awhile to happen. Which means, I'm pretty well sunk for this year." He crunched despondently on his rice cracker. "I mean, I can't avoid those jerks for an entire year, can I?"

Tower tried to imagine an entire year of skulking about in the hallways and behind tall kids to avoid the bullies, and found the entire scenario terribly depressing.

"I am on your side, but those dumb guys will get bored and move on to someone else whether you get a house or not," Sky said.

Tower was unconvinced. He was sure that he was the target because he was so weird, his family was so weird, and where they lived was the weirdest of all. The odd thing was, Sky was easily as weird as he was, weirder actually, and he never got singled out and picked on. The guy's name was Sky Blue for crying out loud, and he didn't even try to look like the back-to-school ads, but that didn't matter. Jeremy and his pals left him totally alone. Not that Tower wanted his best friend to get tormented like he did; he just wanted the world to make sense.

But even without the Jeremy factor, he wanted that house. He wanted the normal way it would make him feel. Was that so wrong? Maybe he wasn't cut out to be a hippie. After all, he didn't choose it, it was chosen for him. Tower's eyes widened, pleased with that thought. That was it. That was how he could explain the house thing to his parents when the time came.

The boys finished their lunches in silence.

Tower managed to dodge out of school ahead of Jeremy's gang and streaked off to the library. He was on a mission and he was not about to let anything get in his way. He needed to check the website and find out the eligibility requirements so he could formulate his plan.

Tower hurried down the streets of the small town and paused outside the quaint red brick library to catch his breath. He didn't want to attract any attention by huffing and puffing. One more deep breath, then he opened the door and sidled over to a computer.

He typed in the web address that he had memorized from the brochure and began reading. He quickly scrolled through all the literature about the organization's mission statement. Maybe adults liked reading all that, but he thought it looked like a bunch of fluff and way too many words to read. Ugh. All he was interested in was the eligibility requirements and the application forms. As soon as he found them, he printed them out and headed to the circulation desk to pay.

"I have six pages," he told the librarian. He fanned them out and offered up his dollar twenty. He couldn't wait to get home and read them and start the whole process of filling them out. That might take a little bit of creative writing on his part. He preferred to think of it as creative writing rather than lying.

Besides, this Neighbor For Neighbor group built houses for people who needed them, and Tower definitely needed one.

Tower rushed home, his mind on all sorts of stuff like counter tops and paint colors and carpeting. Odd how he had lived his whole life before now never even thinking about these things and for the last two days had barely been able to think of anything else. He hoped he didn't have one of those TV medicine diseases. What was the one where you thought or did something over and over? OCD, that was it. He didn't want that. Even though everyone seemed so happy in those medicine commercials with butterflies and everything, he didn't want some crummy disease. Great. Now he was obsessing about having an obsessive disease.

"Think of something else, Tower," he told himself. It was no good. It was like when you get some stupid song stuck in your head and the more you tried to think of a different song, even going so far as singing Happy Birthday, it stuck with you like glue all day. And it was always a stupid song, wasn't it? Never a song you wished you would actually hear played on the radio. That's how it was for Tower right now. He couldn't think of anything but worrying about obsessing about a house. Geez, he was turning into a fruit loop.

CHAPTER NINE

Tower didn't have a chance to examine the pages he had downloaded until later that evening, after all his chores were completed and the family had finished their dinner. His father had looked at him strangely during dinner a few times, even though Tower tried his best not to look anxious or squirmy. He wondered if his face was giving him away. He still hadn't had a chance to practice his facial expressions in front of a mirror, so that had to be it. He probably had some freaky eye twitch.

As soon as he could, he excused himself from the table and escaped from the scrutiny of his father's gaze. He took a detour on the way to his room to check out his face in the bathroom mirror. He stood in front of the mirror and looked at his reflection. He looked like he always did. He made himself think about being sneaky, and watched his reflection carefully. There, did he blink a few too many times? And did his mouth make a little grimace? He couldn't tell.

In his room, Tower sped through the application until he got to line twenty-three, which asked for the household's adjusted gross income as reported on last year's 1040 tax return. Tower's pen hovered over that for a second, wondering if he could make something up, and if so, what number would he pick? He needed this to be believable. What would a family of four need to earn to look needy, but not ridiculously so? After a few minutes of waffling over what to do, he decided to use his parent's actual tax records and copy down the information and let the powers that be decide his fate. That way if the organization ruled in their favor, then Tower would have nothing to feel guilty about. They would deserve that house.

This thought cheered Tower up immensely and he jumped off his cot. He had barely made it to the door when he realized he had no idea where his parents kept their tax records. They didn't exactly have an office. He ran through the contents of each room in his mind. Kitchen, living room, bathroom. Those were all the common spaces in the trailer, and Tower knew those areas like the back of his hand. The only place left was his parent's room, which at this moment contained his parents. It killed Tower to think that he couldn't finish filling out the paperwork.

But there was nothing else to do but wait for a good opportunity to go snooping around in his parents' room. The thought of that made shivers run up and down Tower's spine. He wasn't afraid of his parents, but he understood there were boundaries of acceptable behavior. Invading their privacy and rummaging through their closets and drawers would not be edging over the boundary, it would be bulldozing across it. Tower squelched the sudden twinge of anxiety by telling himself that it was for the good of the whole family. His parents and sister needed this house as much as he did, only they didn't know it yet. On that happy thought, Tower settled down with his homework.

The next day, Tower rushed home from school. He opened the front door and called out.

"Mom, I'm home." A little smile danced around Tower's mouth when no one answered. The stars must be in alignment. He knew he had beaten Teeny home, but there was never any telling about his parents' schedules. If they had real jobs, he would know their schedules and be able to plan accordingly. Tower wondered if they had any idea how much more difficult this commune decision of theirs made his life. They probably told themselves, "isn't it nice we have so much time with the children?" without even considering that one of their children would need them to have predictable work hours, so he could sneak around. Wow. Saying it like that made him feel like a worm. And maybe his parents were smarter than he was, and actually did consider that.

Tower could picture them putting their heads together years before they even had any children and laughing at the thought. "No kid of ours is going to be able to pull the wool over our eyes if we live out here."

Tower shook his head, and told himself to stop all this silly time wasting and get a move on. He hurried down the hall to his parents' room, and stood looking about. This shouldn't take long. The sole hiding place he could see was the built-in dressers along the far wall.

He rummaged through the first drawer carefully, but became impatient when he saw it was all clothes. He opened the next one in a hurry and ran his hand through it. Also clothes. Come on. This was ridiculous. How could they have so many clothes? They wore the same thing every day. Panic was beginning to set in as he opened the final drawer. Aha! Papers. At first he was elated, then dismayed at the unorganized jumble that met his eyes. How was he going to find anything in that mess?

He riffled through the papers with increasing urgency, then finally spotted a manila envelope labeled 'Taxes.' Bingo! Tower couldn't believe his luck. It was almost like a sign. It was taking effort to get this project going, but so far nothing had been insurmountable.

"Tower? Are you home?" his mother called. How had she managed to enter the house without him hearing her? Clomping up the metal stairs to the front door should have been ample warning. He had to get out of here.

Tower looked frantically at the manila envelope then stuffed it inside his shirt, shoved the drawer closed, and hurried out of the bedroom to the nearest place he would have a legitimate right to be. The bathroom. A corner of the envelope rode up out of the neck of his shirt. Tower poked at it quickly and got a nasty paper cut on his neck. He rubbed at the sharp pain as he got one step into the bathroom.

"There you are." His mother was right behind him. From the tone of her voice, Tower didn't think she had seen where he had come from. Even so, he was reluctant to turn around. He was sure his mother would be able to spot the manila envelope under his shirt if she got close enough. And if she saw he had a bleeding injury, she would jump into nurse mode, with her face mere inches from the pilfered tax forms. That was too risky.

"Uh, Mom. Do you mind? I gotta go."

"I wanted to remind you to pick Teeny up from macramé lessons," his mother replied as she wandered back down the hall.

"Yeah, sure. I remember now." Tower shut the bathroom door and drew a deep breath. That was close. Tower examined his neck and saw there was a little line of blood. He turned on the faucet and dabbed at the scratch. He waited a few more seconds, then flushed the toilet for good measure. He didn't want to arouse any suspicion in case his mother was still in earshot.

He opened the door, peered down the hallway, then made a dash for his room. He looked in dismay at the clock, then stuffed the manila envelope under his bed and headed out to pick up Teeny from her lesson.

Later that evening, Tower finally had a chance to get back to his forms. He spread the tax return on his cot and studiously filled the application out, line by line. A knock on the door broke his concentration and he looked up in annoyance.

"Tower. It's time to go," his sister called.

"I'm busy."

"Dad said to get you."

"Beat it. I said I was busy." Tower tried to refocus on the forms, until another knock on the door disturbed him again.

"Come on, boy. It's time to go." This time it was his father. Tower decided to pull out the homework card. His father put a great deal of importance on education.

"Sorry, Dad. I've got homework. Can't go tonight." Tower held his breath.

"Now no arguing. You know Thursday nights are family nights. You should have done your homework earlier."

Tower stuffed the paperwork under his pillow furiously, and emerged from his room to face his father.

"I had to pick Teeny up from macramé class, remember?" Tower tried to explain, but his father interrupted him by clapping a hand on his shoulder.

"You're a good brother. Now come on. The more time we waste here, the longer it'll take us."

At this point there was nothing to do except go along, but Tower was in a foul mood. It was unfair. Here he was, trying to do a good thing for the family by getting them a house, and at every turn he was thwarted by events beyond his control. He was going to have to stay up late tonight and finish filling the forms out. He was bound and determined to get them in the mail tomorrow.

Tower climbed in the decrepit family sedan where his sister and mother were waiting and hunched down. He used to like family nights, but that was when he was a little kid and didn't know better. Other people went bowling or played Monopoly or rented a movie, but not them. No way, not them. They went salvaging.

"I don't know why we have to do this." Tower's bad mood was getting worse.

"You know Friday garbage days are the best. Folks around here know better than to throw away anything useful," his father said.

"I mean, why do we have to do this at all? Couldn't you get an ordinary job?" Tower regretted the words as soon as they came out.

"That wasn't for me. This family doesn't lack for anything, does it, boy? Haven't I done all right by us?" Tower felt bad at the sound of hurt in his father's voice. He sighed.

"Yeah, Dad. We're doing okay. I'm kind of in a bad mood."

"One of those days, huh?" His father sounded sympathetic.

"Yeah, I guess it is." One of those days. It felt like he was having more than his share of 'one of those days.' He forced himself to shake it off and not spread misery to the whole family.

He turned and looked out the window at the neighborhood they were driving through. Large shade trees lined the street and every lawn was immaculately manicured, with landscape lighting illuminating the gardens. Tower noticed all this but it was the houses themselves that captured his attention. They were enormous, with fancy brickwork and gracious balconies. Tower tried to imagine living there, but couldn't seem to bring a clear picture up in his head. Funny, he had no trouble at all imagining living in a house like Rosemary's. Her house felt warm and cozy. These houses made Tower feel like he was looking at art; beautiful but untouchable.

The sedan cruised to a stop in front of a house that had extra debris piled next to a garbage can.

"This looks promising. Everybody out." The family hopped out, and Trivia handed out work gloves. Teeny plopped herself down in front of a box of broken tiles, while Bo immediately homed in on an old-style, square wash basin stuffed full of discarded items. He quickly emptied it out and stepped back to admire it. He gave out a low whistle.

"This is a beaut. Give me a hand, boy."

"Lift with your legs," Trivia cautioned. Tower had heard that lecture so many times that it was now instinct for him to squat, using his strong thigh muscles any time he had to lift anything heavy. Maybe that's why parents said the same things over and over; so kids would turn it into instinct. Parents had so many tricks up their sleeves kids didn't stand a chance. The only option open to them was to grow up.

Tower put on his gloves and squatted down on his side of the wash basin. Suddenly a floodlight glared on. The family froze in place; Tower still hunched down awkwardly.

"Who's out there?" A middle-aged man in expensive pajamas and robe strutted down the cobblestone driveway. Bo straightened and greeted him.

"Hey, man. I saw this old sink, here. Could put it to some use if you don't mind?" Tower couldn't believe how calm his father sounded. Not much seemed to bother him. Tower envied him that. He was the total opposite of his father, anxious and bothered by most things. Especially now, being caught by a homeowner with their hands in his garbage. How embarrassing. Tower tried to stay hidden behind the sink.

"James? What's going on? Who are these people?" The shrill voice of a woman split the air and sent Tower cringing the way you do when someone scratches their fingernails on a chalkboard. He peeked from around the sink and saw an elegant woman standing on the porch. Tower was surprised to see she was wearing high heels with her flowy white nightgown.

"Everything's okay, dear. This guy just wants our old sink." The man tried to reassure his wife.

"You're not going to let him steal from us, are you? I'm calling the police." Her high heels clicked furiously as she stormed back into the house.

Bo raised his hands in a gesture of peace.

"Hey. Buddy. I don't want to cause any trouble. We'll put it back."

Tower was relieved to hear that because he was sure the shrieky-voiced lady was on the phone to the police, and he would just as soon be long gone from this place before they showed up. He stood up and started to replace the items in the sink.

"Hey, Dad? What's going on?"

Tower knew that voice. He looked up, and there, standing in the middle of the driveway was Jeremy. The boys locked eyes for what felt like an eon. An evil little smile crossed Jeremy's face. He nodded at Tower.

"Howard."

Of all the houses, on all the streets in this town, wouldn't it be Tower's luck that they would end up scavenging from Tower's arch enemy?

"You want the sink? It's all yours," Jeremy's father offered. "It was a great sink for giving the dog a bath."

"Thanks, appreciate it," Bo replied. He gestured to Tower to help him load it into the car.

"Enjoy your bath. See ya tomorrow," Jeremy said. There was an unmistakable threat in that statement. The two fathers were totally oblivious to it, but it was there plain as day, and Tower knew it. Jeremy turned and followed his father up the driveway, but right before he entered the house, he gave a little wave.

Tower wished he could hop in the car and drive to Mexico, or maybe convince his parents to home school him; anything that would keep him from having to deal with the fallout from this stupid night. He should have tried harder to convince his father that he needed to stay home, then this whole sink fiasco would never have happened. He bet Jeremy was inside that fancy house of his filming him or taking pictures or calling all his friends to come watch.

Tower had to get that blasted sink loaded into the car or this night would never end. He hefted his end with a grunt and he and his father waddled to the car. They struggled to fit the sink into the trunk, but despite shifting it this way and that, there was no way to fit it in and allow the trunk to close. Tower had done enough geometry and knew enough about angles to know this. His father, however, must have either skipped all his geometry classes or he was an incurable optimist, because he would not give up.

"Push on that end, boy," his father coached.

Tower shook his head. "It won't fit, Dad. Can't we put it back and go home?" Tower was desperate to get out of here. He kept looking up the street for the police. He avoided looking at the house, because he was not about to give Jeremy the satisfaction of a clear shot of his face. All he needed was to have this episode posted on some website.

"It'll fit." Bo kept at it, but he finally stepped back and said, "I sure wish I had a bungee cord or some rope. Trivia, you drive. I'll have to ride in back and hold the top down. It's not that far."

"You've got to be kidding me. Dad, no. Please." Tower couldn't believe his eyes when he saw his father wedge himself in the trunk and pull the lid down; one boot covered foot dangling out. He waited for his mother to object but she was already climbing in the driver's seat. He couldn't understand his parents sometimes, but he wasn't about to stick around outside Jeremy's house arguing. He helped Teeny with her box of broken tiles and got in the car.

"I'm glad we're getting a dog. I always wanted a dog. I'll call him Sugarplum," Teeny announced as she fastened her seat belt. Tower's bad mood erupted.

"We're not getting a dog. And what the freak kind of name is Sugarplum for a boy dog, anyway?" Tower couldn't help himself. This evening was a disaster for him, but for the rest of his family, it seemed it was business as usual. Tower stared out the window, wallowing in pure misery.

"Tower. Watch your mouth." His mother looked in her rear view mirror. "Oh, dear." She put on her right turn signal. Tower saw a reflection of flashing lights coming from behind them.

"Oh, geez. I don't believe this." Tower hunched down in his seat, mortified. Why did his father decide to ride in the trunk? Why? Tower knew it was a bad idea, but no one listened to him.

Teeny took off her seat belt, knelt on the back seat and looked out the window. "There's a police officer getting out of a car. He's carrying a flashlight."

Tower tried to shush her from giving a play by play account. What did she think she was, a sports announcer? Maybe in Teeny's world that's exactly what she thought she was, or maybe a news reporter. "News reporter? Oh, no, please don't let there be any news reporters," Tower prayed. He got up on his knees to see what was happening for himself.

The police officer approached their vehicle cautiously and tapped on Bo's foot with his flashlight. Then Tower and Teeny couldn't see anything else, because the trunk opened and their view was obstructed. Tower sunk back down in his seat. He hoped his father wouldn't get arrested, but most of all, he hoped this would be over before the reporters showed up and they were on the television news, or blasted across the front page of the morning paper. That would make tomorrow a truly hideous day. It was going to be bad enough as it was.

After a few agonizing minutes, his father got in the passenger side of the front seat. He waved at the officer.

"Nice guy. He had a piece of rope. Drive slowly, though," he instructed Trivia. "Seatbelts fastened?" His father turned and smiled at them as if nothing had happened. Here Tower's whole life was ruined in one evening and his father was clueless. It wasn't fair.

CHAPTER TEN

Tower huddled in his bed and tried not to cry, but it was no use. Thoughts of all the things that were wrong with his life kept flitting across his brain. He lived in this crummy trailer, on this crummy commune and his family seemed to go out of their way to embarrass him. The Jeremys of the world would always pick on him as long as things stayed the same. Tower tried so hard to be normal. The thought of all the work he had done to look normal and act normal overwhelmed him and sent a new round of tears coursing down his face. He sniffed loudly.

"You crying?" his sister asked. Those dratted cardboard walls were absolutely useless. A guy couldn't even feel sorry for himself in the privacy of his own room.

"That's my allergies." He sniffed a few more times to convince Teeny. Next thing he knew she started singing Christmas carols. In September for crying out loud.

"Knock it off, Teeny. I need this stupid, egg-sucking day to end. So I can go to school tomorrow and have that be the worst day of my life." Even the thought of school tomorrow sent a pang through his stomach, and he curled into a ball to make it go away. He heard the crunching sound of Velcro, and saw Teeny's hand emerge from a little window cut out in the cardboard wall between their beds. Their father had cut that out when Teeny was little so Tower could hold her hand when she was scared or lonely.

Teeny's hand wiggled. Tower looked at it. It wiggled again. Tower rolled onto his back, sighed and took her hand. She squeezed it.

"It'll be okay. You'll see." She squeezed his hand tightly until Tower squeezed back. He wasn't about to tell his father, but this little window thing actually worked. Who would have guessed that holding the hand of his eight-year-old sister would make him feel better? Not that he thought that it would change anything at school, but maybe, at least, he could get a little sleep.

As soon as the alarm clock went off the next morning, Tower felt his heart start pounding. Then his stomach twisted into a knot as he remembered the events of last night. He heard the rest of the family begin moving about. Teeny's voice trilled with one of her songs. Tower couldn't tell if it was a real song or one she had made up. He squeezed his eyes shut in an attempt to return to sleep. That was all he wanted to do right now. Escape back into unconsciousness and hopefully stay there forever.

Weren't there people out there who retreated to their beds for years, when things got to be too much for them out in the real world? Tower thought that maybe they had the right idea. And his father couldn't find fault with it, because that's how he had brought Tower up. Not to fight. In the wilderness, didn't animals resort to the fight or flight instinct when they were in danger? Well, that's exactly what Tower was doing, escaping to his burrow, which in this case was his bed.

Tower was so busy with this line of thought that he didn't hear his mother until she poked her head in his room.

"You're running late, honey."

Tower groaned. Luckily he was still curled in a ball, so it looked like he had a stomachache. "I don't feel so good."

His mother entered the room and laid a hand on his forehead.

"No fever. What's wrong?" She sat on the edge of his bed. This made Tower nervous because she was looking at him with all those motherly powers of observation eyes. He hoped he could pull this off.

"Uh. Everything hurts. And I feel all throw-uppy." This wasn't exactly a lie. He did feel all throw-uppy. He groaned again, and grimaced, then worried that his bad facial expressions might give him away. He rolled over into his pillow so his mother couldn't see his face.

"Hmm. I'm keeping you home from school today. I want you to rest."

"Okay," Tower replied in the tiniest, weakest voice he could muster. It must have sounded good to his mother, because she tucked in his bedspread and left him to sleep.

Once again, Tower scrunched his eyes closed and tried mightily to return to the oblivion of sleep, but his body defied him.

Later that afternoon Sky showed up toting his grungy backpack. Tower was never so glad to see someone than he was to see Sky. It was one thing to stay in bed all day when you were truly sick, but it was another thing entirely if you were faking it. Tower could not remember ever having been this bored in his life. Besides, he had an errand he needed Sky to do for him. He had finally finished the application and he wanted it to go out in today's mail, but there had been no opportunity to sneak out of the house and do it himself. His mother was big on rest when you were sick. She always said things like, "rest now, so you can run tomorrow."

Sky plunked down on the corner of the bed, far enough away not to catch something.

"Dude? You really sick? Your mom made me swallow echinacea just to come in here." Sky shuddered.

Tower sat up. "Sorry, it's what she does." Tower pointed over to the crate-as-a-nightstand that was covered with a mish-mash of ginger products. There was a can of ginger ale, a few gingersnaps, some ginger capsules and a cup with slivers of yellow-brown root floating in water. Sky wandered over and picked up the cup.

"Gross. What's that?" Sky set down the cup like it was contaminated.

"Ginger root tea. Great for nausea. Unless you're faking it, then it makes you sick. The ginger ale is okay, though."

"Yeah, I figured you were faking."

"How?" Tower was curious. By the time they had gotten home last night, it had been too late to call and tell Sky Blue what had happened. .

Sky opened his backpack, and pulled out a paper bag.

"I wasn't just given homework to bring to you today." He reached into the bag and pulled out a black banana peel. Held it up and dangled it so Tower could see, then tossed it toward the garbage can. He reached in again and pulled out an empty milk container, an apple core and a stub of a pencil. "Oh, yeah. And this. Missy thought you could use it." Sky dropped a clothespin on the bed. "For your nose."

Tower grabbed the clothespin and flung it across the room. "I get it!" He slumped back down on his bed.

"At first, I didn't know what was going on. You know they weren't about to tell me. But then some of the girls couldn't stop giggling while they were looking for something gross to add to the collection, and I got it out of them. Of all the places to go salvaging. What stinky luck."

"You're telling me. I can't ever go to school again. Want to run away?" Tower began to percolate the idea in his brain. Running away would solve everything. They could go and do whatever they wanted. No worrying about dodging bullies; no family rules to bog them down. Yeah, that sounded perfect.

"Nah, we don't want to do that. Can you imagine never having another of Lucifer's pizzas? It's not the end of the world."

Sky tried to reassure him. "They'll forget all about it by Monday. You'll see." Not that Sky actually believed it, but he had to calm Tower down. What Sky didn't tell Tower was how Jeremy had had a crowd around him most of the day, and with each telling of the story, it got more and more embellished. The kids thought it was the funniest thing they had ever heard. The last he heard, Jeremy had Tower's family living in a dumpster and eating from whatever they could dredge up from beneath them. But there was only so much truth you could tell your best friend. Sometimes you had to fudge a little.

"Yeah, maybe." Tower hoped Sky was right. "Hey. I need a favor. I've been cooped up here all day and this has to go out in the mail today." He pulled out an envelope from under his mattress. "The post office doesn't close till five. I'll make it up to you, I promise." Tower gave Sky his most appealing look.

"Sure. No problem." Sky took the envelope and the couple of bucks that Tower handed him. It wasn't that far to the post office, and he felt sorry for his friend. It was the least he could do.

Tower stayed in his room a little longer after Sky left, then headed out to the living room. This faking it thing was a real drag. You couldn't simply spring up good as new, you had to ease into it, or the next time you needed to fake you wouldn't be believed. Tower hoped he would never have to fake again, but he couldn't predict the future. The years between eleven and eighteen, when he could legally make his own decisions might be particularly rough. He might need to do this again, but it was Friday and they were heading into a weekend. He didn't want to waste his weekend stuck indoors drowning in herbs, so it was time to convince his mother he was getting better. He sunk down onto the couch and tried to look almost like his usual self.

"Hi, Mom." He used a voice stronger than the one from this morning. His mother looked up from what she was doing in the kitchen.

"You sound better. Hungry?" Tower was starving. Gingersnaps and soda crackers didn't take up much space in his stomach.

"Mmm. Maybe. Yeah. I think I could eat something." Tower was pleased with the way that sounded; not too eager to cause suspicion, but interested enough that his mother would bring him some food. Tower never realized how complicated communicating was. There were a lot of subtle nuances to observe. It wasn't merely about words; it was the tone you used, your body language, everything. A shoulder shrug in the wrong place, or a too chirpy tone of voice, could derail your whole message and land you in a world of hurt. No wonder humans were the only creatures to master language. It took too much time and effort. Animals were too busy trying to eat or avoid being eaten to care about communicating with each other.

The weekend passed more quickly than Tower would have liked, but at least it was pleasant and uneventful. Tower's mother made him sleep in late on Saturday, and then when she was convinced he wouldn't relapse, she released him to his father's care with a warning that he not overtire Tower. Tower was secretly pleased at all the fussing. He was tempted to milk it a little, but he didn't want to be stuck in the house again, so he jumped right in to help his father. They, along with Sky, pulled nails out of old boards Bo had salvaged from a historic building that was undergoing renovation. To Tower they looked like any other boards, but his father looked at them like they came over on the Mayflower.

"Look at the grain." Bo ran his hands up and down the wood. "And the patina." Tower didn't even know what patina meant. He could look it up in the dictionary, but he would probably forget before he got around to it, so he did the quick thing, and asked his father.

"It's the coloring or shine something takes on as it ages. New wood, new metal doesn't look like this. This wood has character, personality." Bo answered. Tower thought that was stretching it a bit. Character, personality? Weren't those human qualities? He didn't see how they could be applied to building materials. Although, when he looked closely at the surface of the boards, Tower had to agree they had a nice patina.

For the most part Tower was able not to think about Monday. Staying busy helped, so did focusing on the positive. He pictured the envelope containing his application, flying through the air, to whoever was in charge at the organization, and getting a big red "approved" stamped across it. With each nail he pulled out, he pictured hammering new ones into the walls of his own house. He smiled dreamily, and caressed the board he was working on. He froze when he saw his father looking at him, until he noticed that his father was smiling at him approvingly. "Oh, he thought I was appreciating the patina," Tower thought. Oh, well, no harm in his father thinking that. Tower smiled back. It felt good to share a moment with his father. Even though, in this case, they weren't exactly on the same page.

By the time Sunday evening rolled around, Tower was in a state of uncontrollable anxiety and worry. He knew there was no way that the kids at school would have forgotten anything in two days. He knew for certain that Jeremy and his friends would remind them if, by some miracle, they had. Tower's anxiety got so bad, that he finally had to go outside and throw sticks in the creek behind their trailer. It felt better to be outside doing something physical, instead of under the scrutiny of his parent's eyes in the cramped living room. Plus, he was tired of bumping his head into all the hanging herbs and smelling like a lavender shampoo commercial as he paced back and forth.

CHAPTER ELEVEN

Monday morning, Trivia decided to drive the children to school. Tower was not sure how he felt about this. He was lazy enough to like not having to walk, but he definitely did not want to arrive at school one second earlier than he had to. Tower dragged out getting ready as long as possible, trying even his mother's usually endless supply of patience.

"For pity's sake, Tower, your shoes are by the front door like they always are. Quit your dawdling and get into the car before the clock strikes twelve and it turns into a pumpkin." Trivia said.

Tower shook his head. Was it any wonder that Teeny was so full of make believe and fairy tales with a mother like that? But he knew his mother well enough to not push her any further. He grabbed his stuff and jumped in the car.

His stomach was in knots. He was not looking forward to this day at all. But if he complained about feeling sick again, he would be subjected to a whole slew of his mother's herbal remedies. Besides, it wasn't like he could put off going back to school forever. He closed his eyes and tried to do some of his relaxation meditations, but was jolted back to reality when his mother slammed the car to a stop.

"I don't believe it! They've killed Mud Bay!" Trivia said. Everyone in the car stared out the windows. What used to be an untouched forestland on the edge of a tidal mud flat was now abuzz with human activity. Cranes lifted the carcasses of trees onto the backs of log trucks, and bulldozers pushed the stumps and branch debris into enormous piles.

Trivia got out of the car, rummaged in the back seat and found a few old coffee cans and yogurt containers. She handed them to the children.

"Quick. Gather as many fir cones as you can."

"Mom. No. I can't be late for school. Not today." Tower stayed in the car.

Trivia ignored him and ran into the middle of the cleared area. She squatted down and inhaled deeply. For a fleeting second an expression of pleasure crossed her face. She clapped a hand over her mouth and nose in horror, then started picking up fir cones as fast as she could. Teeny hopped down and helped.

Tower was torn with indecision. He loved this forest. He hated to see it bulldozed into oblivion, but he had to get to school on time today. There was nothing to do, however, except to help his mother. He knew how she was when she was in the throes of environmental fervor. He got out and began collecting as many fir cones as he could reach from the side of the road. He was undoubtedly going to be late to school, but he was not going to give the kids one more thing to tease him about by showing up covered in mud.

The bulldozer's roar was louder. Tower looked up and saw the bulldozer bearing down on his mother and sister. He called out but his voice was overpowered by the noise of all the engines. He had to get their attention or they were going to be flattened. He tried jumping up and down and waving his arms furiously. No one noticed. The bulldozer was only a few feet away from his family. Finally the operator noticed and hollered at them. Tower couldn't hear a thing, but he saw the guy stick his head out the side window. He didn't think his mother heard anything either, because she didn't even look up, let alone move out of the way.

The operator gave up trying to talk and put the bulldozer back in gear. The bulldozer moved closer. Tower thought it looked like the driver was aiming for his family. He didn't know what to do. Even if he ran as fast as he could, he wouldn't reach them before the bulldozer did. He had never felt so helpless.

Teeny looked up, saw the bulldozer, and grabbed at her mother in terror. Trivia, shaken loose from her obsession, saw the gravity of their situation and scooped Teeny into her arms. Still clutching her stash of fir cones she ran for the car.

The bulldozer operator pulled to a stop and shut off the engine. The man jumped down and charged after Trivia, hollering the whole way.

"Lady, you and your kid could have been killed. I'm calling the cops."

Trivia stood her ground. "Go right ahead. And I'll tell them you were intentionally driving toward us while we were minding our own business gathering fir cones." There was a stare down, then the man turned away.

"You got your lousy fir cones, now get lost. This is private property, and you were trespassing." He got a few feet away.

"Murderer," Trivia said softly. The man turned quickly and shot her a disgusted look, but Trivia ignored him and ushered the children into the car.

"Mom, we could have been killed! Why did you do that?" Tower asked.

"I had to save the forest, Tower, and get some seeds. Those were native trees." Trivia sounded sadder than Tower could ever remember, but he couldn't see why those particular trees were so important. They lived in Washington State. There were trees everywhere. Weren't they the same as the ones his mother almost got herself and Teeny killed over? If she wanted to plant a tree, couldn't she go into the woods around the commune to pick up fir cones? Tower had been scared to death that she and Teeny were going to be pancaked. All for a few ordinary fir cones. Geez.

Tower's heart rate and rhythm had finally settled into a near normal state by the time they arrived at school, when he felt it pick up the pace again. This day was going to be the death of him. He checked his watch and was dumbfounded to see that he was a few minutes early. The drama at Mud Bay had felt like an eternity. Time was funny like that sometimes. Tower said good-bye to his mother and fled the car before she could do something silly like kiss him.

Tower took his seat without making eye contact with any-one, and fiddled with his backpack in order to distract himself. Finally the bell rang and Mrs. Jones began her lessons.

Almost immediately, Tower heard a few stifled giggles behind him. Tower felt his poor, burdened heart sink like a Bermuda Triangle ship. He resisted the urge to look, so he didn't know that Jeremy had started passing a brown, grocery-sized paper bag around the room. Several of the children placed items in the bag before handing it to the next student.

After a few more giggles, Mrs. Jones turned around. All she saw was a sea of innocent faces on the children as they copied the notes from the white board. As soon as she turned to the front, the children resumed passing the bag until it reached Matt, who folded over the top and taped it shut. Then he whipped out a pink bow and slapped it to the front of the bag. This time there was outright laughter, not giggles, and Mrs. Jones turned to face the class sternly.

"What is going on?" As she asked that, the bag was given a shove and it slid into the middle of the aisle. Mrs. Jones marched over to the bag. "What is this?" The students squirmed uncom-fortably in their chairs, trying to avoid her gaze.

"It's for Tower." A few of the students said simultaneously.

"It's his birthday," D.J. said.

Tower furiously shook his head. "It's not my birthday." He caught Sky's eye, pleading with him. Sky interpreted this message loud and clear.

"Nope. It's not," Sky backed him up.

Tower wished that Mrs. Jones would accept it at that and get back to the lesson, but he knew better than that. Teachers never left something like a bag with a big pink bow on it, uninvestigated. Mrs. Jones picked up the bag. She walked over to Tower's desk and placed it square in the middle.

"Tower. It seems the children may have been mistaken about your birthday, but since they went to all the trouble, you can open it now." She smiled at him.

Tower smiled back, and placed the bag on the floor.

"I, um, I'll open it at home. It's a family rule." This time he didn't shoot Sky a look, but Sky vouched for him anyway.

"Yeah, they have lots of family rules."

But Mrs. Jones was not about to be swayed. "I think it would be good manners to open it now, so you can thank your classmates. I'm sure your parents would agree," Mrs. Jones said.

Tower could not think of any more excuses, so he picked up the bag and placed it on his lap. He opened it and looked inside, then slapped a fake smile on his face and turned to the class.

"Thanks everybody." He rolled the top down on the bag, and started to place it underneath his desk, but Mrs. Jones intercepted it.

"Let's share with the class, shall we?" Mrs. Jones opened the bag and took out the items. There was an old pair of sneakers, a one-inch stub of a candle, a used toothbrush, a partly full bottle of bubble bath and a pink scrubby as well as other old, grungy things. The torture of watching the endless parade of junk being pulled out of the bag was almost too much for Tower to bear. Finally, Mrs. Jones reached the end. She looked at the items on Tower's desk and frowned.

"This seems to be some kind of a joke. We don't have time for this nonsense. Eyes front and center." She strode to the front of the classroom. Tower stared at the stuff on his desk. He was tempted to march over to the garbage can and dump it all in, but instead he tossed it back into the bag and shoved it under his desk.

Sky Blue leaned over and tried to comfort him. "At least it wasn't gross stuff today," he whispered. Tower glared at him. There may not have been eggshells or coffee grounds, or used tissue, but a stinky pair of tennis shoes and a spit-encrusted toothbrush was disgusting enough in Tower's mind. And the pink scrubby and bubble bath was downright insulting. That was like calling him a girl, and Tower didn't think he deserved that. Sure, his family reclaimed discarded items, but there was nothing Tower had done that was at all girly. His depression at the situation was starting to turn into anger.

As soon as the bell rang, Tower slammed his 'gift' into the trash and fled out the nearest door. He could hear a few snickers behind his back, but no one spoke to him directly. In the mood he was in, he would have likely forgotten all his family's teachings and belted the first person to say "boo" to him.

Once at home, he was restless with pent up energy. No one else was home, which was a good thing, because he didn't want to take out his bad mood on anybody. After awhile, he left to see if Sky wanted to hang out. He peeked into the shed, but Sky's bike was still missing.

CHAPTER TWELVE

Tower poked around in the shed a few minutes, killing time, when he spied a can of WD-40 and grabbed it down from the shelf. He remembered the squeak of Rosemary's screen door and decided to see if she wanted him to fix it. He needed to do something. Tower looked at the rusty bikes. It didn't matter if anyone saw him riding one now, so he swiped at the seat with an old rag, then climbed on and rode off. He had forgotten how much fun it was to be on a bike. He liked the feel of freedom and the wind in his face.

His mood had lightened considerably on the ride to Rosemary's. He hopped off the bike and climbed the stairs to the front porch. For a second, an attack of nerves immobilized him. Tower squelched it down and rang the doorbell. Rosemary opened the door and smiled at him in surprise. Tower was happy to hear that the door still squeaked.

"Tower. Nice to see you again."

"I thought, um, I could fix this door for you now." He held out the can of WD-40.

"Sure. That would be nice." Rosemary said.

Tower held the screen door and squirt some oil on the hinges. He swung the door back and forth a few times, to make sure it spread out effectively, then tested it. The squeak was gone. Rosemary looked at it, suitably impressed.

"There, that'll do ya." Tower was proud of his handiwork. Maybe there was a little of his father in him after all. Rosemary tested the door.

"Thanks. I didn't realize how much that was getting on my nerves. You did a good job." Rosemary smiled. "Do you want to come in?"

Tower bounded through the door, happily. This was following the script he had practiced on the way over here. Tower did that a lot. He would picture a scenario, and how he wanted it to come out. He even went so far as to have imaginary conversations, acting out both his lines and the other person's. Most of the time, when he put it into play, it did not go the way he had planned. It was like the other person hadn't received a copy of the script and did not follow the lines that Tower had written for them. It was highly disappointing.

But right now, Rosemary seemed to be on the same page. Tower didn't know if he was getting better at his imaginary script writing, or if this was just a fluke. It didn't matter; finally something was going his way today. He supposed it was kind of strange that he wanted to hang out with a lady he guessed was about as old as his father, but Tower felt comfortable here. Besides, he wanted to find out more about the Neighbor For Neighbor home building project.

He wandered around, trying to figure out how to bring up the subject. On other days, he would have been able to come up with some creative way to broach the subject, but this day had sucked out all the mental energy he possessed.

"Uh. You know that house building thing? I, we, applied for one." That was close. He almost blew it. Eleven-year-olds did not get approved for a house of their own. He needed to make sure it looked like his parents were the driving force in this.

"That's great," Rosemary answered.

"Yeah, we really need a house. Soon."

Rosemary was sorry to disappoint him, but she didn't want his hopes unrealistically high. "I'm afraid the process takes quite awhile, Tower," she said.

Tower was discouraged. "Yeah. Maybe a house wouldn't change anything, anyway." He sighed, long and loud. It must have been louder than he thought, because Rosemary rushed to try and make him feel better.

"If you come with me this weekend, we can see about getting you started on your hours."

Tower was confused. "Hours?" What was she talking about?

"You read that part of the brochure, right? Everybody has to put in a minimum of five hundred volunteer hours before they qualify," she explained.

Tower was stunned. He had been in such a hurry to print out the application, that he hadn't read everything on the Internet. He had scrolled through what he thought was a bunch of legal mumbo-jumbo; now it looked like he had missed something important. He looked around for a pencil and paper.

"Can I use these?" he asked.

Rosemary nodded her consent and Tower furiously scribbled some multiplication problems. He looked up in disbelief.

"If I work eight hours, every Saturday and Sunday, it'll take me more than seven months. And that's not even my house?" This was looking bad.

"Your parents' hours count, too." Rosemary hastened to reassure him.

"Uh. They're not...they're not able to help." Tower slumped down into one of Rosemary's chairs. Why was everything so hard? Every time he thought he could fix his life, something beyond his control unraveled all that he had worked so hard on. He barely noticed when Rosemary sat down on the couch across from him.

"Oh. I think the hours are cut for the disabled," she offered helpfully.

"Great." Tower wondered if being a hippie was a disability. No way. There was probably a law for even thinking that.

"You hungry?" Rosemary got to her feet and headed into the kitchen. Tower followed her and watched as she made some sandwiches. He was rather disappointed to see that all she took out of the fridge was cheese. He couldn't count how many cheese sandwiches he'd eaten in his life. Thousands. He must have betrayed his emotions, because Rosemary stopped what she was doing.

"You do eat cheese, don't you?"

"I eat anything. Ham is good." Tower remembered the last time he had had a ham sandwich. It was wonderful. There was something about the salty flavor that had his mouth watering just thinking about it. His eyes lit up when he saw Rosemary retrieve some from the refrigerator.

"Sorry. I thought you lived on that commune. Aren't you a vegetarian?" She cut the ham in paper-thin slices, then piled them high on the bread. Ordinary wheat bread, not the kind with all the seeds in it that his mother always bought.

At least she had given up on making her own bread; those had come out like bricks. If you made the mistake of taking a normal sized bite, it would take about ten minutes and a whole glass of water to get it down. On homemade bread days, you learned to take teeny bites and have a full glass of water standing by. None of the family ever told his mother how horrible her bread was, because one of their family rules was that you had to be gracious about the food you were served. And while his parents didn't go so far as to make the children clean their plates, they had to at least try everything served to them. They called it adventure bites. Everyone heaved a sigh of relief the day his mother announced that baking wasn't her thing, and from now on they would be buying their bread from the co-op.

Tower noticed that Rosemary was still waiting for an answer. "What? Oh, yeah. I'm a vegetarian. I, uh...I like meat, too."

"Ah. One of those meat-eating vegetarians." Rosemary turned away to conceal her amusement. She reached into the cabinet and pulled out two plates. She assembled the rest of their snack and handed one plate to Tower. He looked at it curiously. There were three segments separating the sandwich, the grapes and the potato chips.

"What's with the plate? Do you work in a cafeteria?" Tower hoped his question did not sound rude. He was relieved to hear Rosemary laugh.

"I can't stand my food to touch, that's all," she answered.

"That's weird." Oops. That was definitely rude, but Rosemary didn't seem to take offense. Tower decided he better eat his sandwich before he stuck his foot into his mouth again. After a few seconds of companionable silence, Tower raised the subject of the house again.

"So, how do I go about getting these hours you were talking about?" Even though it looked like an almost insurmountable quest, Tower was determined to continue with his plans for a house. Maybe it wouldn't change anything this year, but Tower was convinced that living in an ordinary house was the answer. He envied other kids who were born into normal. They didn't even have to think about it. They had normal parents with normal jobs and normal homes. They had it so easy. Tower may not have it easy, but he did have the willingness to work. He waited eagerly for Rosemary's answer.

"I'll make a few calls; get you started this weekend. Show up here ready to work." Tower was elated. Having something to look forward to would make the rest of the week go by faster.

He thanked Rosemary for the snack, picked up his can of WD-40 and hopped onto the bike. This day had gotten off to a shaky start, had a rotten middle, but the end was looking up. Tower was even getting fond of this rusty old heap. Of course, he would never admit that to Sky. There were some thing a guy had to keep to himself. Tower soared through the neighborhood, swooping in and out of driveways to catch a little air. The sturdy bike seemed to enjoy it as much as Tower did.

Tower returned the bike to the shed and wiped it down with the rag. A little more of the rust came off. A little elbow grease, and some new paint, would perk this guy right up. Tower added that to his mental list of things to do and headed up the gravel drive to his home.

A major project was underway in the kitchen. A variety of recycled containers filled with dirt lined the counters. Teeny sat on the floor surrounded by dirt and fir cones. She bashed at them with a small rubber tipped mallet and sifted through the debris for the seeds, which she deposited into a canning jar. Trivia sat next to her with a large bag of organic potting soil. She filled the recycled containers with the dirt, and set them on the counter. She looked up when Tower entered.

"Yogurt in the fridge for dinner," she said.

"No thanks, I'm not hungry." Tower was thankful that Rosemary had fixed him such a substantial snack if all they were having for dinner was yogurt. Yogurt wasn't very filling.

"That was a command, not a request. Eat." Trivia stood up and fetched a yogurt from the refrigerator. "Do you have any idea how many of these containers we need?" she asked. She handed Tower the yogurt. At least it was Lemon Burst, his favorite. Tower got a spoon. It was easier than arguing. Tower's father arrived home and surveyed the scene.

"Early start this year?" He was referring to Trivia's habit of starting seedlings for her vegetable garden indoors every spring. Trivia looked up at him sadly.

"We're going to grow more trees. And the scoopy thing is not going to get them," Teeny piped up.

"Oh, Bo. I'm a horrible person. They murdered a forest, and for a second, I actually enjoyed the smell. Of dead trees," Trivia said.

Tower wondered how his father could follow this train of thought, since he hadn't been there to witness the bulldozing incident, but his father seemed to understand his mother without question. It must have something to do with being married so long. Tower had seen them do this before; even finish each other's thoughts. It was kind of eerie.

Bo ruffled Trivia's hair and kissed her on the top of her head. "It's okay, doll. You're not the one with sap on their hands. So, it's yogurt for dinner tonight?"

Tower handed him a spoon. Tower felt sort of guilty that he had gotten a ham sandwich when all his father got was a yogurt. Not guilty enough to confess to his parents about his meat-eating spree, though.

CHAPTER THIRTEEN

Saturday finally arrived. Sky and Tower were in Tower's room getting ready for their day of construction. Clothing was strewn across Tower's bed. He pulled out one of his father's old flannel shirts.

"How about this?" Tower asked Sky.

"Yeah. That could work."

Tower put it on over his t-shirt. It hung down to his mid thighs, and the sleeves swallowed his arms entirely. He rolled the sleeves up. "You don't think it makes me look sissyish?" Tower gave a final tug at the shirt.

"Nah," Sky pronounced, "It's perfect." They left the house and headed for the shed. Tower looked around the shed for the hard hats.

"They should be in here somewhere." His father had most of the tools mounted on pegboards around the perimeter but Tower didn't see the hard hats anywhere.

"Wall la." Sky held two hard hats aloft.

"It has a V," Tower corrected him.

"Va la? Huh, uh. I don't think so." Sky shook his head vehemently.

"Voila. Vwall ah." Tower said with a French accent.

"Whatever. I found them. Let's go." Tower gave Sky a critical look and frowned at his bright, white overalls.

"Wait." Tower opened a paint can and daubed some on each of their clothes. Sky jumped back in protest.

"What did you do that for? These are brand new." Sky wiped at the paint.

"I want it to look like we've done this before. Anyway, you got them at Salvation Army."

"So? I like them. And I liked them unpainted on better," Sky said.

Tower peered out the shed door. "Coast is clear. Let's go." They left the shed at a dead run, not wanting to get caught and have to explain what they were up to.

It was one of those perfect mid-September days in Washington State. The kind that made anyone planning on moving out of state before the endless rainy season began pause and reconsider their decision. Tower and Sky made it to Rosemary's house in record time. Tower was surprised that Sky offered to help on the house project. It would help him get his volunteer hours in much sooner with a second person's help. Which meant that Tower would be moving from the commune that much sooner. Which is why he was surprised Sky was willing to help.

"Hey, um, thanks for coming with me," Tower said as they were waiting on Rosemary's front porch, hard hats and battered tin lunch pails dangling from their hands.

Sky shrugged. "What else would I do on a Saturday except hang out with my best friend? Where did you tell your Mom you were going today?"

"The pool. She's going to pick us up there at five." Remembering the lie made Tower feel a twinge of guilt, but he told himself it was for the good of the whole family. His parents may not be open to the idea of moving now, but once the house was done and they saw how nice it was, they would forgive him this lapse of honesty. He hoped. You never could tell with parents.

Sometimes they got mad at the smallest things, and sometimes when you thought you were going to get into trouble, they simply smiled and told you it was all right.

"I still think you should tell her we're volunteering." That's what Sky had done. And his mother beamed at him and called him a real humanitarian. Sky thought that meant he liked humans, which was true, and if it made his mother happy and his best friend happy, well, that was good enough for Sky.

"Nah. I'm afraid if I start talking about it at all, I won't be able to stop, and I'm not ready for big explanations." Tower rang the door. "Besides, she's got enough on her mind."

Rosemary answered the door. "Be right with you." She disappeared back into the house.

Tower took this time to tell Sky Blue about the other morning. "You should have seen her. There we were gathering fir cones, and the bulldozer is getting closer and closer, and the guy's like hollering, "lady get outta here, it's dangerous..." Tower didn't noticed Rosemary standing in the doorway. "...and Teeny was terrified. It was crazy." He looked up and noticed Rosemary.

"Oh, hi. This is my friend, Sky. He can donate his hours, can't he? I mean he's like family."

Rosemary shook Sky's hand, warmly. "Sure you can have Sky's hours. And since I already have my house, you can have mine, too."

"This is a Neighbor For Neighbor house?" Tower looked at the house in surprise.

"Yep. Thought you knew." Rosemary started toward the car. Tower stifled the urge to ask more questions, as the boys got into the car. On the drive to the construction site, Tower continued to wonder about Rosemary. What did she do for a living? She had never discussed a job with him. How had she qualified for a house? Tower would have guessed she was middle class, but then, before he discovered this house program, he had never before thought about upper, middle or lower class. If he thought about it at all, he would have said he didn't know any rich people or any poor people. Everyone seemed to be working people, same as their family. Except not the same as their family, because their family was too weird for words. Geez, this was confusing.

It was a good thing that they arrived at the construction site, because Tower's head was spinning. Before too long, Tower wasn't thinking about anything at all. That was one of the best parts of physical labor. You could either over work your body or your brain, but not both at the same time. Tower's brain was concentrating on not hitting his thumb with the hammer, and how good the sun felt beating down on his arms now that he had abandoned the flannel shirt. He wasn't worrying about why people did what they did, or said what they said, or who was in what income class. He wasn't worrying at all.

Rosemary, Tower and Sky worked as a team on one section of the house. Everyone framed out their wall on the ground first then raised them vertical, where other volunteers would secure them. Tower was surprised at how quickly the skeleton of the house took shape.

"When you have your home study, make sure you tell Mrs. Clark you've already started on your contributory hours," Rosemary said.

Tower froze; hammer in mid-air. "Home study?" Did his voice actually squeak?

"It's a formality. I let her know about your folks. The fact that they're disabled will speed things along," Rosemary replied.

Sky shot Tower a questioning look. There was no mistaking that it was a questioning look. Tower shot him back a desperate tell-ya-later look. He hoped Sky wouldn't pick now to lose the ability to read his face, because Tower sure didn't want him blurting anything out.

"Uh, when is this home study?" Tower asked. He tried not to sound panicky.

"No telling. I'm sure she'll call first. Are you okay?"

Tower smiled at her weakly. "I'm fine."

Rosemary walked away.

Tower sunk to his knees and moaned. "Oh man oh man oh man."

"Disabled? Tower, you can't lie about something like that. God or lightning or something will strike you down," Sky said. He pounded a nail to demonstrate, but missed the nail and hit his thumb. Hard. Sky danced around with his thumb in his mouth, the way you do when you've just hit your thumb with a hammer, but don't want to draw attention to yourself by screaming like a banshee. "Ow. Ow. Like that, but worse."

"I know, but I didn't lie to her. She sort of assumed. And I… sort of let her." Tower defended himself.

Most of Sky's pain had subsided. "You want me to pretend to be your dad?"

For a split second Tower considered this insane idea. "That would never work. You couldn't pass for… a day over thirteen."

"Hey, thanks." Sky Blue strutted, pleased at the compliment.

The foreman, Carl came rushing over. He was a hefty, bald guy with a plastic Popeye pipe clenched between his teeth.

"Didn't hurt yourself, did ya boy? Cause we have to report every teeny-weeny little thing to OSHA. Those government safety guys can be a real thorn in my side." Carl spoke rapid-fire from around the edge of the pipe, every word sending a few bubbles drifting about his head.

Sky formed a fist around his sore thumb and lied. "I'm fine."

"Good news, good news. Cause the last thing I want to do is fill out a bunch of forms in triplicate for those lily-handed suits to gloat over." He inhaled deeply and immediately coughed and spluttered. He pulled a handkerchief out of a pocket and sent a little bottle of bubbles flying. Still coughing into his handkerchief, he chased after his bubbles, leaving the boys staring at him in amazement.

"What's with that guy?" Sky asked Rosemary, who had returned.

"Oh, Carl. He's trying to quit smoking. He couldn't take the patch or the gum, so he came up with that."

"Weird." Tower stared after him thoughtfully.

"Whatever works." Rosemary didn't seem at all bothered by Carl and his weird solution. Tower used to think he was the only weird one around. Well, including his whole family, of course. Now he was beginning to see there were a lot of people who were weird or, if not weird all the time, did some weird things sometimes. This realization made him feel a little better.

After they said goodbye to Rosemary at her house, Tower and Sky hurried the few blocks toward the YMCA. Before they got there, Tower pulled Sky underneath a large stand of bushes.

"Hey. What the...?" Sky protested. Tower shushed him, and found the Hefty bag he had hidden here a few days ago on his way to school. He thrust a pair of swim trunks and a towel at Sky. Sky stared at them in disbelief.

"You have got to be kidding me! There is something wrong with you, you know that?" Sky pushed at Tower. "At least turn around."

It was impossible to stand up under the bush, and the boys were scratched and out of breath by the time they had struggled out of their construction clothes and into the swim trunks. When they were finally changed, Tower poked his head out of the bush and looked around, then nodded at Sky. They crawled out from under the bush.

The boys were worn out by the time they arrived at the YMCA. They practically collapsed on a low stone wall as they waited for Tower's mother to come pick them up. They sat in a companionable silence, or maybe they were too tired to talk. Tower watched the sprinklers hiss left and right across the immaculately groomed lawn, and he thought how pointless it was to water the grass so late in the season. In a few weeks, nature was going to take over the watering and wouldn't stop till next July. Staring at the sprinklers, Tower was all of a sudden struck with a thought.

He jumped off the wall and dragged Sky off as well. He pushed Sky into the middle of the sprinkler's path. Sky yelped as the cold water hit him, then he charged after Tower and pulled him in the water. Sky shoved Tower's face right into the sprinkler head. Tower had to hold his breath against the force of the water, and just when he thought his lungs would burst, he must have done some fancy karate move, because next thing he knew he had flipped Sky onto the ground. They wrestled around on the lawn, until a gardener hollered at them.

"Hey, you hooligans! Get off that lawn!"

The boys could tell by the tone of his voice that he was serious. They beat a hasty retreat back to the stone wall. Sky toweled bits of grass off of himself and glared at Tower. "What did you go and do that for?"

"We weren't wet." Tower explained. "That would have raised some suspicions."

Sky sighed. "You know, it's going to get cold soon. I am not taking my clothes off under a bush, and running through the sprinklers, then."

"I know, but don't worry, I'll come up with something." Tower tried to make his brain think, but it wasn't responding at the moment.

CHAPTER FOURTEEN

Dinner was simmering in a crock-pot when they arrived back from the pool. Trivia lifted the lid and peeked in, then announced that dinner would be ready in about a half an hour. Tower headed off to his room to get out of his wet clothes. The one thing worse than being in wet clothes, was being in wet clothes in cold weather. Tower knew he would have to think of something soon, but he was more worried about the home study. He decided to give his brain a break, and not try to force anything. Maybe this would be one of those times when something magical would pop in out of the blue. A guy could hope, couldn't he?

In the kitchen, Trivia stripped the seeds and dried blossoms off of stalks of lavender into a large bin. Teeny sat at the table and spooned the lavender seeds from a small bowl into silky eye masks, and pinned them closed. Trivia would finish them off by sewing the ends, and put them up for sale in the co-op store.

Bo clomped in and kissed Trivia and Teeny on their heads, before sitting down and taking off his heavy work boots. He stretched out into a chair. "Great day. I got a lot of stuff for our..." He glanced at Teeny. "...project. Pipes and some good solid planks." He smiled.

Trivia smiled back at him, then looked closely at him and her smile changed to a frown. She pulled off her work gloves. "Look at you," she scolded, "you're all sunburnt." She snipped off a frond of an aloe plant, slit it open and placed the two halves, gooey side down, on Bo's burnt forehead. "Skooch it around, okay?"

She had returned to the lavender when Tower entered.

"Hey, everybody."

Trivia looked up. "Not you too. How did I miss that? Sit down, young man."

Tower, not sure what he had done, obeyed instantly. He was relieved to see his mother approach with an aloe frond. He took the pungent aloe frond, and slid it up and down his arms. "I'm being slimed. This is disgusting."

"But it works. How many times have I told you to put sunscreen on?" She sighed.

"Too late now," Teeny said. "You have to smell like armpit, and I get to smell like lavender." She danced around the room, waving a sleep mask around.

Tower smelled one of his arms. "It doesn't smell like armpit."

"Whatever. I still smell better than you."

Trivia went to the fridge for a Brita pitcher and poured two big glasses of water. She brought them to Bo and Tower.

"Drink. And when you're finished with those, get another. You didn't know enough to protect yourself from the sun; I'm guessing you didn't drink enough water, either. Men." She turned away and started to serve up dinner. Tower and his father exchanged sheepish looks. Tower added "bring sunscreen tomorrow" to his mental list.

"You take such good care of us," Bo said to Trivia.

"Oh, no you don't. No making nice," Trivia replied, but Tower could tell she wasn't truly mad.

Monday morning Tower was lost in thought as he trudged to school. He heard the sound of running feet pounding behind him and immediately tensed.

"Hey wait up." Sky caught up to him, out of breath.

"No bike?" Tower questioned.

"Thought I'd walk. I'm sore all over." Sky groaned.

"Yeah. Me too." Tower was still preoccupied.

"What's bugging you?" Sky asked. That was the thing about best friends. They could sense your mood in a heartbeat.

"I still haven't figured out what to do if that Mrs. Clark wants to come over. How am I going to keep her away from my parents and still get her to okay the house for me? I don't want all the work we put in this weekend to be for nothing," Tower fretted.

"So you're the only one that matters? It's all for nothing if some other deserving family gets a house, but you don't?" That's the other thing about best friends. They weren't afraid to point out your flaws.

"That's not what I meant. I meant, we've come this far. I don't want a little thing like a home study to wreck it all."

"I told you this would never work. I told you no one was going to give you a house for nothing. I told you..."

"I know, I know! You told me everything. Well, if you know everything, tell me what to do now." Tower challenged Sky.

"Sorry, dude. I've got nothing," Sky said, unapologetically.

The rest of the way to school, Tower kept his brain going a mile a minute, trying to find a workable solution. He could intercept Mrs. Clark and keep her away from the rest of the family. Maybe he could pretend to live in one of the other houses on the communes. No one ever locked their doors. The philosophy was what's mine is yours. Yeah, that was it. If anyone were home at his house, he would use Nelson's house. The main problem was going to be catching Mrs. Clark right as she drove into the commune so Tower could guide her to where he wanted.

CHAPTER FIFTEEN

Tower fidgeted in his chair, watching the second hand on the clock move in slow motion. The last few days had been pure agony for him. Not because of the trash the students continued to bring him. That was still embarrassing, but he had kind of gotten used to it. No, it was because that Mrs. Clark lady had still not shown up for the home study. And Tower had been ready for her. He had beaten everyone home the last few days; he'd even snuck over to Nelson's and made sure the door was unlocked. And still she didn't show. It was driving him crazy.

Finally the bell rang, and Tower nearly bolted out of his chair. He was almost to the classroom door, when he heard Mrs. Jones call out to him.

"Tower? May I have a minute?

Tower squirmed with impatience, but he couldn't be rude to his teacher. "Uh, sure."

Mrs. Jones waited until all the other children had left before she turned to Tower who was fidgeting uncontrollably. If she made him wait one more minute, he would burst.

"I can't help but notice that the other kids seem to pick on you a lot. Is there anything I can do to help?" She sounded genuinely concerned.

Any other day, Tower may have stayed and talked to her, but today he was in a hurry. "No. Everything's fine. Honest. I gotta go now." He anxiously grabbed the door handle.

"You know all this junk they keep bringing you? Turn it around on them," Mrs. Jones suggested.

"How so?" Tower was baffled.

"Think on it. You'll come up with something." Mrs. Jones encouraged him.

Tower gave her a quick smile. Great, just one more thing to have to think about. Before she had a chance to say anything else, Tower fled out the door.

✳ ✳ ✳

Trivia finished sewing the last of the sleep masks and tossed it into a full basket. She rubbed at her tired eyes and stretched her shoulders. She got up as Teeny bounded in from school, and gave her a kiss.

"Hi, honey. Good day at school?"

"Pretty good. I got to feed the silkworms. Then they'll make a cocoon and spin cotton into gold." Teeny proclaimed.

Trivia was too tired to try to correct this fanciful story. "That's nice. Listen, hon. I was up all night getting these masks finished. I'm going to take some Valerian and lay down for a little while, okay? Your snack is in the fridge." Trivia headed down the hall.

"Okey doke." Teeny happily went to the fridge for her snack. She found a piece of peanut-buttered bread wrapped around a whole banana, and pulled it out. She took the banana out of the bread and began to slice it, then cut the bread into small squares. She hummed a little tune while she worked, then arranged it all in a neat circle on a plate.

"I am quite in the mood for a tea party," she said with an English accent. She rummaged around way in the back of a cupboard and finally found a bag of sugar. She liberally poured sugar on top of the peanut butter; then after a moment's hesitation, on the banana slices as well. "Lovely." Teeny admired her creation.

✳ ✳ ✳

Tower rushed past Sky Blue, not even noticing him waiting on the stairs.

"Hey. Wait up," Sky stood up.

"Hurry. I need to get home in case that lady comes today," Tower said.

Sky groaned. "We've run home every day for a week. I'm getting tired."

Before they could move, Jeremy, Matt and D.J. sprung out from behind some bushes and stood in menacing poses at the bottom of the stairs, trapping Tower and Sky.

"Ooh. He's tired, Howard," Jeremy mocked.

Tower stared at them in disbelief. He didn't have time for this. It's not like there was ever a good time to be bullied, but today was particularly bad. Tower tried to edge past them, but the three boys formed a wall.

✳ ✳ ✳

A brown, mid-sized car pulled to a stop outside Tower's trailer. Mrs. Clark got out of the car and looked about with trepidation. She adjusted her tan skirt and pasted a sympathetic smile on her face, then knocked on the door.

Teeny, with a food-smeared mouth, answered the door and poked her head out.

"May I help you, madam?" she asked, still using her English accent.

"Uh, is this the home of the Adam's family?" Mrs. Clark asked, as Teeny examined her from head to toe.

"Yes. Won't you come in and join me in a spot of tea?" Mrs. Clark hesitated, then stepped inside.

✳ ✳ ✳

Jeremy reached out and placed both his forefingers directly beneath Sky Blue's eyes, then he pulled down slightly, creating bags.

"Yep. He's tired," Jeremy said. The three boys laughed.

Sky was scared. He tried backing up, but his leg was wedged against a stair.

"Leave him alone," Tower said. He hoped that would get Jeremy's attention off Sky.

✳ ✳ ✳

Teeny ushered Mrs. Clark into the living room, where she had her tea party set up on a colorful cloth in the middle of the floor. She plopped down and patted the floor next to her, encouragingly. Mrs. Clark gingerly lowered herself to the floor.

"Is your mother home?" Mrs. Clark asked.

Teeny rolled her eyes. "Of course. Do you think I'd let a total stranger in the house if I were alone? Although you do seem to be a respectable lady with sensible shoes."

Mrs. Clark looked down at her brown loafers. "Thank you." They were sensible but stylish, she thought, and matched her outfit perfectly. She remembered why she was here. "Could you go get her, please?"

"Oh, that won't be possible. She had a spell of the vapours, don't you know, and took her valerian, and off to bed she went."

94

Teeny stuffed one of the sugared bananas in her mouth, then poured some fluid out of the teapot into a cup, and handed it to Mrs. Clark.

Mrs. Clark didn't quite know what to make of this odd little English-accented child. She accepted the cup.

"The crumpets are delightful," Teeny said as she ate another piece of bread.

"So she took this Valium and went to bed?" Mrs. Clark tried to get to the bottom of this situation. She had forms to fill out.

"I quite expect her to be out like a baby the rest of the afternoon."

"I see." Mrs. Clark was becoming alarmed. "And your father? Where is he?"

"Oh, hither and yon. I'm sure I haven't a clue." Teeny smiled at her.

✳ ✳ ✳

Sky Blue had managed to back up a few stairs when Tower distracted Jeremy. He was glad to have a little distance between him and the bully. Tower thought that distance and a little height would show a sign of strength, so he turned his back on Jeremy and started to join Sky on a higher step. Jeremy reached out and grabbed at some hair at the back of Tower's neck.

"What, no pony tail?" Jeremy taunted.

"I cut it off so your mother could use it as a wig." Tower was secretly pleased at this quick comeback. Usually it took hours of him replaying a conversation for him to come up with something that good.

Jeremy, also, was shocked at this uncharacteristic response for a split second then he became enraged.

✳ ✳ ✳

Mrs. Clark looked around the room and frowned when she saw numerous bottles of vodka, containing the next batch of echinacea tincture, lining the counter. She got to her feet.

"I must be going now. Thank you for... your hospitality." She turned for the door.

Teeny took one of the peanut butter squares and offered it to her. "Crumpet for the road?"

Mrs. Clark recoiled at the sight of the slimy, sticky glob. "No thanks. Uh, late lunch."

Teeny accepted this explanation with good grace and shoved the bread in her mouth.

✳ ✳ ✳

Jeremy was furious at the insult Tower had directed at his mother. How dare he insinuate that his mother wore wigs? Tower had to know that insulting someone's mother was grounds for getting pummeled into the ground. "I'm going to kill you," he said.

As Jeremy started to charge, Tower spotted a teacher approaching. He shouted, "No! I won't get into a fight with you." He put his hands at his sides and silently prayed that the teacher had heard him.

Jeremy advanced with his arm cocked back ready to punch. "Your funeral."

Tower braced himself for the pain that was about to land somewhere on his face. He closed his eyes. When the pain didn't arrive, he squinted one eye partly open and took a peek.

The teacher had a hand firmly clamped on the back of Jeremy's neck, and was marching him back inside the school building. Matt and D.J. had bolted as soon as they saw the teacher barreling their way. Tower caught Sky's eyes and they both breathed a sigh of relief.

"That was close," Sky said. "I'm shaking."

"Yeah. Now you see why I've got to get a house? As long as I live in the commune, Jeremy will see me as a target." Tower didn't see the look of sadness and fear that crossed Sky's face as they hurried down the street, anxious to get home.

✳ ✳ ✳

Tower and Sky turned into the commune driveway and were passed by a brown car exiting with a crunch of gravel. Tower broke into a run. He burst into the trailer and looked around. Teeny watched him calmly, finishing up the last of her snack.

"Teeny. Who was here?" Tower prayed that maybe it was a census taker, or some kind of sales person.

"A lady with brown shoes wanted to see Mom. I told her she was taking a nap," Teeny answered, without the English accent.

Tower was afraid to get his hopes up. "That's it?"

"Yep."

"This is important. Exactly what did she say? Did she say she was coming back?" Tower urgently questioned her.

Teeny took an impossibly long amount of time to answer his question. Tower had to restrain himself from shaking her into the next county. Which wasn't like him to even be tempted to physical violence. It must have been a little of Jeremy rubbing off on him. He shuddered at the thought, then forced himself to wait patiently for Teeny to answer.

"She didn't say. She asked for Mom, she asked for Dad, then she said thanks for your hospitality. I was very hospitali–hospitali-LICIOUS." Happy with her word, Teeny gave Tower a sweet smile and licked sugar off her lips.

✳ ✳ ✳

Mrs. Clark dialed her cell phone. "It's a sad situation. Absentee father, and the mother has some kind of substance abuse or anxiety problem." She paused to listen. "You say this young boy has been working on his volunteer hours? It sounds like he's the one keeping this family going. Go ahead and move them to the top of the list. They clearly need a house."

CHAPTER SIXTEEN

Tower and Sky waited around outside their classroom as the rest of the class entered. Tower had a rolled up poster board under his arm.

"You think this will work?" Sky asked.

Tower shrugged. He had a new plan he was going to set in motion today. The home study had left him feeling optimistic. It had been two weeks, and the lady with the brown car and brown shoes had not returned. So Tower had put his mind toward solving one of his other problems.

Tower entered the classroom and walked up to Mrs. Jones. "Can I have a minute?" he asked.

She nodded and Tower unrolled the poster board. There was a picture of a homeless shelter, and a list of needed items, such as socks, toothbrushes, coats and blankets.

"Hey, everybody," Tower called out to the classroom. "I want to thank you all for contributing to my drive for supplies for the homeless."

The kids exchanged bewildered glances.

"While it's great to reuse stuff, it saves the planet and all that, some of the things you've brought in are a little too used to be, ya know, donatable," he continued.

A few of the students squirmed with embarrassment.

"So, instead of doing what you do for our food drive, bringing in that disgusting can of okra or whatever it is you don't want your mom cook…" Tower smiled back at the laughter that brought, "…let's try to bring in some great stuff. Coats, blankets, socks," he paused to get the point across, "unused toothbrushes."

There was more laughter at that, and one girl hung her head down in shame. Tower hoped this was what Mrs. Jones meant when she said turn it around on them, because it was all he could come up with. He hoped, at the very least, it would stop the endless supply of garbage he had been dealing with.

Mrs. Jones gave him a little nod of approval, as Tower hung up the poster.

"That sounds like a wonderful class project. Thank you, Tower."

Tower returned to his seat, his head held high. A few of the kids actually smiled at him as he passed their seats. That was a good sign, he thought. Things were starting to look up.

✳ ✳ ✳

Western Washington State was not known for spectacular fall colors. Sure, the leaves changed colors, but not with the intensity that other regions enjoyed. The color that was most associated with this area was gray. Dark gray mornings and evenings with driftings into medium or light gray mid-afternoons. Also, there was almost always some type of moisture involved. Mist, drizzle or full-on rain. Tower could never understand it when the weathermen would say something like, "rain turning into showers." Rain was rain. Why didn't they only forecast something that was outside the realm of normal, like, "sunny, with temperatures into the seventies?" They could save a lot of television airtime if they did that.

Luckily, The Neighbor For Neighbor house had gotten it's roof installed prior to the onslaught of fall weather, and the crew had moved indoors.

Tower, Sky and Rosemary struggled with a large sheet of drywall. They finally got it centered and the boys held it in place.

"Okay. Now don't move. I've got to take a little break," Rosemary teased. The boys groaned. Rosemary laughed and drove in the drywall screws. Once the wall was firmly anchored they stepped back and stretched their sore shoulders.

"You guys ready for lunch?" Rosemary asked. She didn't have to ask twice. Construction was hard work and they were starved. It was a good kind of hungry, where you knew that the calories you were going to eat were going directly to fuel your body for the rest of the day's work.

Tower looked up as a lady approached Rosemary.

"Excuse me. May I have a word, Rosemary?" Mrs. Clark asked. The two women moved out of earshot of the boys.

"Which one is the Adams boy?" Mrs. Clark asked.

"The one closest. Why?"

"I just wanted to see him. I'm quite concerned about this family. The little sister was rather strange. She was eating big globs of pure sugar. And there were Vodka bottles all over the counters." Mrs. Clark replied. They looked over at the two boys seated with their backs against the newly hung wall. They opened their lunch pails then both boys stared for a second inside Tower's pail.

Mrs. Clark continued, "I can't decide whether I should report them to Child Protective Services."

Rosemary hurried to reassure her. "Let's not do anything drastic yet. I'll keep my eye out."

"You do that, but please keep me informed. It is my duty to report any suspicions of child endangerment." Mrs. Clark said as she was leaving.

Meanwhile, Tower and Sky were mesmerized by Tower's lunch. There was a large carrot that had been scored with partial slices and scorched up its length to resemble the bark of a palm tree and a green pepper that was hollowed out and carved. Then Tower found a note that said, "Place carrot in middle of hummus." Tower looked in the pail, and pulled out pita bread smeared with hummus and edged with thin slices of green pepper. He took off the plastic wrap, set it down on the plastic plate that was included in his pail, then stood the carrot in the middle of the hummus. He consulted the note again; took the green pepper and stuck the hollow side on top of the carrot to complete the palm tree. Tower stared at this creation in disbelief.

"She's nuts." He said, as Rosemary rejoined them. She looked at him with worried eyes.

Sky couldn't take his eyes off of Tower's fascinating lunch. "Cool. You have an oasis."

"Yeah. What do you got?"

"Peanut butter and jelly. Trade?" Tower nodded thankfully and pushed his artsy lunch over.

"That's got to be the most creative lunch I've ever seen. And it seems nutritious." Rosemary said.

"Yeah, isn't it cool? Tower gets stuff like this all the time." Sky said as he scooped up hummus with a ring of green pepper. "Yum."

Rosemary looked again at Tower's lunch. It was definitely unusual, but not necessarily the work of a woman whose mind was unbalanced. She may have unfulfilled dreams to be a caterer, or a three dimensional artist. Rosemary didn't know. One thing she did know was that although she was not going to prejudge Tower's mother, she was glad that Mrs. Clark hadn't seen the oasis. She was one of those women that had a very narrow view of what was normal, and a very expanded view of what was her business. Rosemary opened her own lunch.

"Good news. Mrs. Clark said the home visit went...well, Tower."

"That was Mrs. Clark?" Tower felt a moment of panic.

"Yes. We start on your house as soon as this one is finished."

Tower could hardly believe it. It now looked like his dream would become a reality. He almost choked on one of the peanuts in Sky's sandwich. "Wow."

"I'll give your Mom a call tonight and let her know." Rosemary offered.

Tower felt his heart pound. He was so close. "Thanks, but I'd love to be the one to tell her." He gave Rosemary the most sincere look he had. He really would love to be the one to tell his mother; just not tonight. Tower was relieved when Rosemary agreed to his request.

CHAPTER SEVENTEEN

The evening air had a definite chill to it and all the residents of the commune were bundled up in coats and had their chairs drawn as close to Lucifer as safety and space would allow. The pizzas came out of the oven hot and bubbling and sent up a cloud of steam around the faces of the people happily munching them.

Nelson plunked his battered chair down next to Bo and got himself some pizza.

"Any news on your project?" Nelson asked.

"Slow going. The bean counters need more beans to count and the paper pushers ain't happy till you've filled out every form created since we stopped writing on walls." Bo replied.

"Makes you wish you could be a hippie and live on a commune, don't it?" They laughed.

"Yeah, ain't that the truth."

"Well, let me know when you're ready to get started," Nelson said.

"Count on it, buddy." Bo nodded at the whole group. "Gonna need every last one of you."

"They'll be there. Everyone thinks your kid is great."

They looked over at Tower. He, Sky and Teeny were having a "who can stretch the cheese out the longest before it breaks and splashes all over your chin and shirt" contest. The children took a bite, and stretched their pizzas farther and farther away from their mouth until the cheese finally pulled off Tower's pizza and splattered all over his face. The children burst out laughing. Tower pulled the cheese off his face and shoved it, skin cells and all, into his mouth.

Bo smiled. "Yeah, he is."

✳ ✳ ✳

Life had settled into a comfortable routine for Tower. He and Sky still pretended to go to the pool on weekends, except now Tower had rented a locker inside the YMCA, so they didn't have to change under the bushes any more. And things had been calm at school the last few weeks. The bullies left him alone and the other kids were actually friendly.

Tower drifted into a daydream that life could be like this all the time. He startled back to the present when he heard Mrs. Jones clear her throat.

"Good morning, class. Before we get started, I want to say how proud I am of you all. Would you look at this?" She gestured toward the huge pile of donated items spilling out of a box under Tower's poster.

The class erupted into wild applause. Sky gave Tower a way-to-go look. Tower beamed.

"You guys did such a great job, we're running out of space. Could you take a load with you after school today, Tower?" she asked.

Tower stared at the huge pile and a lump formed in his throat. "Uh, sure." He stared at the pile again. It seemed even bigger this time. He slumped down in his chair. What happened to that happy feeling he had a few minutes ago? Was there some life manual that he had never been given that said something

106

like, "don't daydream in class about how good you have it?" If so, he was lodging a complaint with the Postmaster General, because his copy must have gotten lost in the mail.

After school, Tower and Sky gathered up armloads of donated items and carefully made their way down the front steps. They could barely see over the tops of their bundles. They struggled down the sidewalk, drawing strange looks from passersby.

"Couldn't you have told Mrs. Jones that we had to get someone with a car before we could take all this?" Sky asked, out of breath.

"I didn't think of it. I didn't think this thing through all the way."

"Duh. How much farther to this shelter, anyway?" Sky asked.

Tower didn't answer.

"Tower?" Sky shifted his load so he could see Tower better. "Tower, where is the shelter?"

"I have no idea." Tower confessed.

Sky stopped in his tracks and dropped his stuff. "Tell me you're kidding."

Tower shook his head. "Nope."

"What about the picture on the poster?"

"I cut it out of National Geographic." It had seemed like a good idea at the time.

"What are we supposed to do with all this stuff?" Sky asked.

Tower shrugged his shoulders. "I don't know. We could chuck it in that dumpster."

Sky backed away. "Uh, uh, no way."

"Hey. I would never have thought of this, if those stupid kids hadn't been bringing me all that junk. This isn't my fault," Tower defended himself.

"Yeah, it is. I thought you were doing a cool thing. If you were going to be a stinking liar, you should have asked for money. It's a lot easier to carry." Sky stormed off.

Tower tried to run after him, but couldn't because of all the stuff. "Hey, wait. Come on, Sky. Don't be like that." Sky ignored him and kept on walking.

After a few seconds, Tower went over to the stuff that Sky had dropped and tried to pick the entire load up. As soon as he got one bag picked up, another one tumbled out of his arms. He kept up this futile effort for a few minutes, then became frustrated and let all the bags fall to the ground. He kicked at the pile as hard as he could.

When he had gotten all his pent up anger and frustration out, he surveyed his situation. No one was going to ride to his rescue so he better figure this out. His arms could only carry so much, and he couldn't leave all this stuff on the sidewalk. He picked up as much as he could carry and walked down the street a little way then set that load down and came back for another. He then took the next load a little way beyond the first, before he set that down and went back to move the first load. In this back and forth fashion, he slowly made his way to Rosemary's.

Tower plopped the last of the stuff at the bottom of Rosemary's porch. He was beat. He would have given his eye-teeth for a wheelbarrow, shopping cart or even a wagon. Which he could have had if he had planned this whole thing better.

Tower rang Rosemary's doorbell and prayed that she was in. He didn't think he had the energy in him to move those bags one more foot. He heard approaching footsteps, then Rosemary answered the door.

"Hi," she said.

"Hi. Uh, I have a problem. I know I shouldn't bother you, but..." the words trailed off, and he shifted uncomfortably.

"What is it?"

The explanation flew out of Tower in a torrent of words that he couldn't control.

"It's the teacher's fault. She should never have told me to turn it around, but I was sick of everybody bringing me ratty shoes or spitty toothbrushes, so I started a drive for the homeless shelter, but I don't even know where any stupid shelter is and now I have to carry all these blankets and coats and stuff, and my arms hurt and I'm thirsty and there's nowhere to store them anyway. And my best friend totally hates me." He was thoroughly out of breath and dejected.

Rosemary, still trying to decipher that speech, spotted the bags at the bottom of her porch. "I have some space in the garage. Buck up. We'll tackle this one step at a time. Okay?" She opened the garage and pointed out a cleared area to the side. "Over there. Come on in when you're done, and we'll get you something to drink. And see? Problem's half solved."

"Everything is that easy for you?" Tower asked.

Rosemary's eyes clouded for a second. "Ah, Tower. Few things are that easy for me."

Tower gathered up the bags one more time and stacked them at the side of Rosemary's garage, then shut the garage door and went inside the house.

He peeked around the door. "I'm done."

Christmas decorations spilled out of a few small boxes. Rosemary was in the middle of stringing lights on a small, living evergreen tree that rested on a corner table. She looked up. "In boy. You're letting out all the heat."

Tower was hesitant to interrupt her, but knew he couldn't stand there with the door open forever. Grownups were sticklers for not wasting heat. He closed the door behind him.

"Sorry. I didn't know you were busy." He stayed by the door, in case it looked like she wanted him to leave. Maybe decorating the tree was a solemn ritual for her.

"No worries. As soon as I get you a drink and let your arms rest, you can help. It's more fun with two people, don't you think?" Rosemary went into the kitchen.

Tower followed her. If she thought it was more fun with two, Tower could only imagine what she would think of the commune's tree decorating party.

Rosemary poured milk into a pan on the stove and turned on the burner. "Cocoa okay?" she asked.

Tower smiled. "That's the way we make cocoa."

"It's the best way. You can't call that powdered stuff in packets, cocoa. Could you get the cups? They're in that cupboard to the right of the sink." She added cocoa powder and sugar to the milk and stirred, careful not to let it scorch on the bottom of the pan.

Tower opened the cupboard and stared at the contents curiously. The shelves were neatly stacked with two of everything. Two bowls, two cups, two plates. He took out the two cups. "You don't have very many dishes."

Rosemary shrugged, and poured the cocoa into the cups. "That's all I need. Too much stuff and it starts to own you. I thought I'd take the Noah's Ark approach."

"What if you have company over and someone brings ice cream?" Tower asked.

"We can use the two cups as bowls."

"What if there's more than four people?" Tower tried to understand.

"You're very 'what iffy today', aren't you? Drink up. We have a tree to decorate."

Tower thought about the Noah's Ark idea. He wondered how far she carried that policy. Did she have two towels? Two spare light bulbs? Two pair of pants? He forced himself away from that train of thought before it led somewhere scary and finished his cocoa.

Tower squatted down on the floor and pulled out tissue-wrapped ornaments from one of the boxes. He carefully unwrapped them and hung them on the tree.

"So, kiddo. You need to find a homeless shelter?" Rosemary asked.

Tower cringed as he remembered his dilemma. "Yeah. How old do I have to be before I stop doing dumb things?"

Rosemary shook her head. "Got news for you. Dumb isn't necessarily something you grow out of."

Tower groaned. "Great. I'm doomed."

Rosemary ruffled his hair. "Maybe. I haven't given up hope on you yet, though. And I happen to know of a nice little shelter."

Tower brightened. "I thought I was going to have to spend all day looking through the phone book." He reached for another ornament. It was a baby food jar lid with a picture of a small boy glued to it. He opened his mouth to ask a question, but Rosemary smoothly took the ornament and hung it on the tree. There was a sad look on her face that made Tower swallow his question unasked.

"Ah, but I am a phone book. Font of all wisdom and knowledge," she answered, her back to Tower.

In no time, the little tree was finished and they stood back to admire it. It was sparsely decorated in a serene and peaceful way. It gave Tower a warm feeling. He reluctantly turned to Rosemary.

"I should get going. Can I leave the stuff for a few days? I'll tell the class the deadline is Christmas break. Then I can be done with this whole dumb thing."

"It's a good thing, Tower."

"Thanks. And your tree is pretty, in a Noah's Ark kind of way." Their eyes met and they exchanged a smiled.

CHAPTER EIGHTEEN

ower arrived home to find things in a minor uproar. It was quite a contrast from Rosemary's quiet home. Trivia was going a mile a minute in the kitchen. She turned when she heard Tower enter and shook a spoon at him.

"There you are. Late again. We've got the tree lighting tonight. And it's our Wanda night."

"Sorry," Tower mumbled.

"Sorry won't string the popcorn. Sit." She turned back to the stove.

Tower joined Teeny at the table, took a needle and thread and a handful of popcorn. He stabbed through the kernels and sped through his pile. His string grew quickly.

Teeny rooted around in the popcorn bowl and examined each kernel closely before she selected it. She then bit off a part of the kernel and added the other piece to a little pile. Tower glanced over at Teeny and saw that her strand was about a foot long.

"What are you doing? We're going to be here till next Christmas," Tower said.

Teeny was completely absorbed in her popcorn. She turned a kernel this way and that, and held it up to the light. "Have you ever looked at a popcorn kernel?"

"Looking at a whole bowl of them now," he said.

"No. I mean really looked at them. Some are crazy with the brown crunchy parts all through them, and then..." She reverently picked one up and showed it to Tower, "...some are perfect. See if I bite this part off, I'm left with a perfect ball. No brown stuff. I save these for later." She chomped the kernel and added the perfect little white ball to her pile of other perfect little white balls.

Tower shook his head in amazement. "Uh, Teeny. Have you seen how big the Christmas tree is? If you go as fast as you can, I promise to make more popcorn later and I'll even help you find the perfect ball-y kernels."

"Okay." Teeny scooped up her little pile and shoved them all in her mouth then began to string as fast as her little fingers would go.

After awhile of speedy popcorn stringing by both children, there were several large strands puddled on the floor and the last bowl was empty. Tower stretched his shoulders and rubbed his neck. His shoulders hurt, his legs hurt and he needed to go stretch out on his bed.

As he got up from the table, his mother snapped the lid on a container and added it to a stuffed picnic basket, then handed the whole thing to him.

"Wanda's dinner. Now make sure you sit with her while she eats, but don't let her dawdle. You still have to eat before the tree lighting."

"Can't Teeny do it? Why can't we have our own tree? I'm tired," he complained.

His mother looked at him closely. "Oh, dear. You do look pale. Hmm, the basket's a little heavy for Teeny." She took a couple of items out of the basket. "The jam's not necessary. It's her favorite, but oh-well. And I guess she can do without the Thermos of coffee."

Tower watched his mother remove items, until the guilt overwhelmed him and he went over and replaced all the food.

"That's okay. I'm catching my next wind now." He put on a brave smile.

"Second wind," his mother corrected.

"No, I've passed that a long time ago. I'm at least on my fourth or fifth by now."

Tower threw on his jacket and picked up the picnic basket and left the house. He clumped down the stairs, and trudged down the path through the woods, toward Wanda's home.

"Yeah, other kids are probably playing video games right now and I'm Little Red Stinking Riding Hood," he grumbled to himself. He almost jumped right out of his skin when someone answered.

"You calling poor old Wanda the Big Bad Wolf?" Nelson teased, on his way down the path.

Tower was embarrassed. "Nah. I didn't mean..."

"Just funning you, kid. See ya tonight."

"Yeah, see ya." Tower waved and headed up the steps to Wanda's trailer and knocked on the door.

Wanda opened the door for him and Tower placed the basket on the crowded kitchen table. He unloaded the items for Wanda, as she eased her aged body down carefully in a chair.

"One thing you can say about your Mom. She sure doesn't skimp," Wanda said. She stared at the plate Tower put in front of her. "Course she cooks some funny looking things."

"That's stuffed eggplant," Tower offered helpfully.

"Well of course it is."

Tower watched as she dug into her food. He didn't know how old she was, but she looked ancient. Most of the people who had formed this commune were around his parents' age, but Wanda was definitely in the grandmother or great-grandmother age range.

"Aren't you a little old to be a hippie?" Tower asked.

"And that's the other thing you can say about your mom. She sure taught you fine manners."

"Sorry." Tower guessed it was a rude question.

"Speaking your mind is the right of the old, boy. It's one of the only things we've got going for us. Wait your turn." She chewed her food, thoughtfully. "When I found this place, it felt like home. Besides, I don't think of myself as a hippie. That's just a word. You people here are my family. If that means we're hippies, well so be it," Wanda said.

Tower looked around at the dusty, cluttered living room and kitchen. Stacks of newspapers as high as Tower was tall created a maze throughout the living areas. It looked nearly impossible for a young person to navigate, let alone someone as shaky as Wanda was on her feet. A recliner in the corner of the room was the only place he could see that could even remotely be described as comfortable. When he thought of the word home, this place would not be even close.

Wanda cackled. "You don't get it do you? That's okay. Run along home and tell your mama this green soupy stuff was good."

"Split pea."

"Well of course it is. Although nothing holds a candle to the ribs Nelson brings. Big drippy things. Practically melts in your mouth." She got a dreamy look on her face.

"You eat ribs?" Tower asked.

"And I'd wear fur, too, if I had a gentleman friend who'd buy me one. But that'll be our little secret, now won't it?"

Tower nodded. "See you tonight?"

"Wouldn't miss it. My age, you take your fun where you can get it."

Tower gathered up the dishes and said goodbye. He thought about their conversation on the way home. He was glad to keep Wanda's secret, since he had a few of his own. He was also glad that she and Nelson ate meat. Well, she hadn't exactly said Nelson ate meat, but surely if he brought her ribs, that meant he liked them too. Meat-eating hippies. It seemed that you couldn't define people by just one word. Human beings were way too complicated for that. He thought about how Wanda said hippie was just a word. A word that Jeremy hurled at him as an insult, a word that Tower was embarrassed to call himself, yet a word that Wanda defined as family and home. Tower thought that maybe she was the one who had it right.

Tower arrived home and ate the dinner his mother had set out for him, then the family went outside to the clearing. Portable tables were set up with plates of cookies, juice and Thermos's of coffee on them.

Bo and Nelson were on ladders on opposite sides of an enormous evergreen tree draping strands of popcorn and cranberries on it. They hopped off their ladders and finished hanging the strands around the lower branches then pulled the ladders out of the way.

"All righty, folks. Have at it." Bo called to the crowd.

The residents began decorating the tree with a variety of natural ornaments like gingerbread men made from birdseed. They clipped on real candles. Tower munched on a cookie and watched the others. He spotted Sky Blue. They eyed each other warily. Finally,

Sky Blue ambled over.

"Hey," Sky said.

"Hey."

"Great tree."

"It's the same tree we have every year," Tower replied.

"You throw all that stuff away?"

Tower sighed. "No," he paused. "That was sure uncool to leave me like that."

"Yeah. Well. Sorry."

"Yeah, me too. Want a cookie?"

"Always," Sky said.

They got cookies from the snack table and ate them without talking. Tower felt better now that he and Sky had made up. They looked up when they heard a scattering of applause. The huge tree was brightly lit with the dozens of candles. They would be allowed to burn for fifteen minutes tonight; then again on Christmas Eve.

"Wow. Cool," Sky said.

"It is now, but by Christmas all the decorations will be eaten up."

Tower didn't see his father come up behind him.

"That's the beauty, son. It used to take my mom forever to take down our Christmas tree," Bo said.

"Yeah?"

"And she wouldn't let anybody help since the year she was in the hospital having my little brother, and my dad had us wrap all the ornaments in toilet paper. The next year, our living room looked like it had been t.p.'d." He shook his head at the memory.

"What a mess," Tower said.

"Yeah. My dad came up with some oddball ideas. And the real kicker was, my mom folded all that toilet paper and put it in a basket and made us use it up. I think it lasted till summer."

"Three square usage unless it's an emergency?" Tower asked.

"Huh?" Sky was baffled.

"That's one of our house rules. Three squares of toilet paper, unless it's an emergency."

Bo laughed. "Come on, boy. Tell the truth. We aren't that unreasonable. It's four squares. You've been cheating yourself out of a whole square all these years."

They all started laughing.

"You have some weird house rules," Sky said.

"That's what I've been telling you," Tower replied as his father ruffled his hair and gave him a squeeze.

"Guitar time," Bo said. He and Nelson drew their chairs up near the tree and strummed out Christmas carols. Tower glanced over at the shimmering Christmas tree, then at his best friend singing carols slightly off-key. It might just be his Christmas spirit kicking in, but he all of a sudden felt content and at peace.

CHAPTER NINETEEN

In the last few days before Christmas break, the stack of donated items grew to an unbelievable height. Tower's heart sunk every time he saw one of his classmates proudly drop off another item. He assumed he would have to carry them to Rosemary's, and his arms ached at the memory of his last back and forth trip. But then out of the blue without him having to think of a way to ask her, Rosemary had offered to pick him up. They had packed up the items from her garage yesterday and were going to the shelter today.

When Rosemary pulled up, Tower was waiting. A few of the classmates even helped load up the car. Amazing. Here he had started the coat drive as a way to put them on notice that he wasn't going to let them keep on bringing him garbage. He would have been happy with that result but it had worked out so much better. Now they actually treated him like a friend. They included him at lunch and picked him for their teams in gym. Yep, it was amazing.

Tower stuffed himself into Rosemary's compact hybrid car. It was a good thing most of the items were soft like coats and blankets because it would have been misery to be wedged in so tight with something sharp and pokey.

They had been driving for about fifteen minutes and a light snow started to fall. Tower wondered where this shelter was.

"Uh, you sure you know where you're going?" he asked.

"Yeah, I'm sure." Rosemary smiled.

"Oh, cause I'm used to getting lost. Course my folks call it taking the scenic route." Tower watched the snow come down more steadily now and thought that this was a perfect way to start Christmas break.

"This was back when everything was normal?" Rosemary asked.

"Huh? It has never been normal at my house." Tower rolled his eyes.

Rosemary tried to be tactful. "I just meant...before your Mom got sick and your Dad...left."

Tower crunched his face up as he remembered his cover story. That was the problem with telling lies. They came up to bite you in the behind when you least expected it. It was way easier to tell the truth.

"Uh." He made a few other grunts and groans while he tried to think of a reply. "About that..."

They turned up a long, tree-lined driveway.

"Sorry. I didn't mean to bring up bad memories. Anyway we're here." She pulled the car to a stop.

Tower jumped out of the car, relieved. For a moment there he was actually tempted to tell her the truth. Lay it all out and take his chances she would see it his way. Thankfully Rosemary interrupted him before he blew it.

Tower looked around and was stunned. They were parked outside a massive brick house with huge wreaths hung on the double front doors. He did a three-sixty, mouth hanging open. This was like no shelter he had imagined.

"Wow. Are you sure this is it?"

He saw a few children and mothers playing in the rapidly accumulating snow.

"I'm sure. Maybe you'll get to meet Mrs. Clark."

Tower hoped he didn't hear that right. He gulped.

"Mrs. Clark? What would she be doing here?"

"This is the agency headquarters as well as a shelter. Hey, buddy. If you don't stop gaping and start unloading, we'll be here all day." She shoved a bag into his arms.

"Oh man," Tower muttered. He held his bundle in front of his face and followed Rosemary inside to an ornate marble entryway.

Wow. They used some expensive materials when they built this place. There were winding staircases on either side of the entry with hand-carved wooden banisters. He would have loved to explore but he didn't want to dawdle. The last thing he wanted to do was run into Mrs. Clark and have to answer any questions. He looked around and spotted Rosemary heading down a hall. Tower hurried after her. Rosemary pushed open a door with her hip and they entered a small storage room. Orderly shelves lined the room. Tower was glad to see that it was empty. They tossed their armloads down onto a long table. The door squeaked open and Tower froze. Don't be Mrs. Clark, don't be Mrs. Clark, he prayed.

"This here is my good friend, Tower. He spearheaded a blanket drive for the shelter." Tower looked up. This didn't look like the lady he saw at the house that day. Whew.

"I am honored to meet you, young man. Most kids your age are all caught up in what they want for Christmas. It does my heart good to meet a selfless youngster like yourself," the lady said.

Tower squirmed. He felt a little guilty hearing her praise him like that, but providing coats and blankets for the homeless was a good thing, wasn't it? So even if he was being a little selfish, other people were benefiting, right? Tower shook the lady's hand.

"Well, I've got some unloading to do. Nice meeting you." He fled before his conscience got the better of him.

He hurried back and forth with loads of stuff, eager to be out of this place. Finally, he deposited the last load.

Tower and Rosemary left the house and walked right into the middle of a major snowball fight. One snowball splat straight into Tower's head, sending icy bits down his shirt. He looked up to see a little girl laughing.

"Ooh, this is war," Tower said, then scooped up a handful of snow and packed it into a ball. He lobbed it at the little girl. He stepped behind a tree to give himself a few seconds to pack another snowball. He was surprised when Rosemary crouched down next to him and began making her own ammunition. They ran, dodging flying snowballs and pelted whoever came within reach. Finally, out of breath and covered in snow, they waved at their rivals and headed back to the car.

"That was fun. Are they all waiting for a house?"

Rosemary shook her head. "Not everyone qualifies."

Tower looked at the people still playing in the snow. "Where are all the dads?"

"Good question. Ready to go?" She started the car. Tower wondered if she didn't say anything more because she thought his dad had left the family and didn't want to hurt his feelings.

Tower was having trouble falling asleep. He gazed through the macramé curtains at the still falling snow. If tomorrow were a school day, it would be called on account of snow for sure. It didn't take much for school to be delayed two hours or canceled entirely. His father had told him when he was a boy in Nebraska school wouldn't be canceled unless there was a true blizzard. He said the snowplows would be out all night clearing the roads. In Washington, there were hardly any snowplows just a few trucks that dumped a lot of sand, which pinged against the bottom of the cars long after the snow had melted. Tower wondered what his father was like as a boy.

"Tower?" Teeny said from the other side of the cardboard wall.

"I'm asleep."

"No you're not. You answered. Tower?" She tried again.

"What?" If he didn't answer he would never get any sleep.

"What do you see when you close your eyes?"

"Dark. Now go to sleep." Tower rolled over.

"You don't see dark with all those red squiggly lines?" She scrunched her face up with her eyes clamped shut.

"That's the blood vessels in the back of your eyes. Now go to sleep."

"I think it's beautiful. Like a kaleidoscope. Especially when you smoosh your eyes with your fingers." She jammed her forefingers into her eyelids. "Now it's all big red and yellow and black." She wiggled her fingers and tapped on her eyelids, and smiled at the explosion of colors.

"That's not good for your eyes," Tower warned.

"Well, I've been doing it all my life and my eyes are fine."

Tower wondered about his sister sometimes. He sighed.

"Tower?"

"What now?"

"What do you think about at night? Do you think about flying horses?"

"Nah. I've been thinking about houses. And families." Tower thought about his mother and father out in the living room. They were on the couch; his mother stretched out with her feet on his father's lap both engrossed in their books.

"Yeah, that's good too. Night." He heard the sound of the Velcro and Teeny's hand reached through the little door.

Tower grabbed it and gave it a gentle squeeze. "Night." He rolled over and snuggled down deep into his covers. He snuck a hand out and pushed lightly on his eyelids. Teeny was right. The changing, swirling colors were mesmerizing. He didn't think he was going to make a habit of it, though.

CHAPTER TWENTY

Tower spent much of Christmas break working on the Neighbor For Neighbor house. He was due to meet Rosemary at ten this morning, so he rushed through his chores at home as fast as possible. The good thing about winter was his chore list was shorter than in summer. In summer there was all the planting, and weeding and harvesting of the herb and vegetable gardens.

He hurried over to Rosemary's bundled in a coat, hat and gloves. The snow had long since melted, so he didn't have to worry about boots. She was backing out of the garage when Tower arrived. They had to run to the grocery store before they went to the house so it was a little after noon by the time they arrived.

There were cars parked everywhere. The closest place to park was a little ways down the street. Tower and Rosemary carried bags of groceries into the house. It took several trips to get them all. Tower plopped the last of the bags on the counter and looked around.

"I can't believe we're finally done." He unloaded the groceries and stocked the new white refrigerator.

At the grocery store, Tower had been surprised when Rosemary had said, "you get the stuff for the refrigerator, and I'll get the cupboard things," and left him on his own. He had absolutely no idea what to get. He thought about what was in the refrigerator at home. There were a lot of vegetables and tofu. He didn't know what a normal family ate but he doubted it included tofu. He got milk, butter, cheese, eggs and yogurt in the dairy aisle, then headed over to the meat counter. He was totally out of his league here. He finally decided to get one package of each species. A chicken, some pork chops, a beef roast and a salmon fillet. That would give them four dinners.

He did some quick math in his head. He had already spent over fifty dollars. Geez, food was expensive and he hadn't even gotten to the fruit and vegetables yet. He wished Rosemary had given him a budget or a list. He headed to the produce and selected some carrots, celery, apples and oranges. He hesitated for a second, then hefted a fifteen-pound bag of potatoes into his cart. It wasn't exactly refrigerator food but he didn't think Rosemary would be shopping in this aisle, and everybody could use potatoes, right?

When the cashier tallied up the final grocery store tab Tower had been shocked. Now he knew why his parents would scold him and his sister if they wasted food. "Don't take more than you can finish," they would always say. He was going to have to pay more attention to that. He put the meat into the freezer and turned to Rosemary.

"All done. This place looks awesome," he said.

"It does. Are you getting excited about your groundbreaking next week?" Rosemary asked.

"It doesn't feel real yet." Tower had to pinch himself to believe that they were discussing his house. His groundbreaking was scheduled to take place the first Saturday in January. He couldn't wait.

"Yeah. Most of the best things in life are like that. It takes awhile to get your mind around it," Rosemary said.

Tower helped Rosemary finish putting the rest of the groceries in the cupboards.

"I didn't know the Neighbor For Neighbor group helped with furniture and food. I think we'll be okay with just the house," he said.

"Don't be silly. You can help your mother choose from a catalog. They won't expect her to go shopping because of her disability."

Tower winced. "That's good, I guess. But they could save the money and help more families if we only took the house," he offered, remembering the huge grocery bill.

Rosemary reached out and gave Tower a breath-ending hug. "I'm proud of you, you know that? Always thinking about others."

Tower squirmed uncomfortably. After what felt like an eternity to Tower, Rosemary let him go. She handed him a few paper bags to fold.

"Here. Fold these bags, then let's hurry outside for the ribbon cutting and key presentation."

Everyone took one last look at the house then grabbed their coats and headed outside. It was a sunny, frigid day and people huddled together to stay warm. Their breaths formed haloes of steam around their heads.

A large ribbon was stretched between the two front porch columns of the new house. A couple of official looking people stood next to Mr. and Mrs. Bradley and their children, Erin and Ellie. The family's coats looked a little too thin for the weather, and Tower wished he had kept a few of the coats that were donated and hung them in the closets.

Tower was excited for them. They had been kept out of the house for the last two weeks so the presentation could have an element of mystery, but before that he had seen how hard they worked on the house. He couldn't wait to see their faces. He bounced up and down on his feet and strained to hear the official.

"On behalf of the Neighbor For Neighbor program, we'd like to present you with the key to your new house." The official handed the woman a shiny new key. "Everyone, let's hear it for the newest homeowners, the Bradley family." The crowd burst into applause then came to a quiet hush as Mr. Bradley cut the ribbon with a giant pair of scissors. The parents guided the children to the front door and Mrs. Bradley fumbled to get the key in the lock. She brushed tears from her eyes and tried again. Finally she got the door open and the crowd cheered again, then everyone swarmed into the house to see their reaction.

Mrs. Bradley immediately went to the kitchen and ran her hands along the counters. She opened the refrigerator and when she saw the food inside, tears coursed down her face. She turned to the volunteers. "Thank you everybody. You don't know what this means to us."

Tower thought she wanted to say more, but couldn't because of the tears. That worried him. He already had tears in his eyes and it wasn't even his house. He looked at Rosemary. "Does everyone cry?"

She nodded. "More or less."

"Great." He didn't want to be sobbing like a little baby when it was his turn to get a house. He was going to have to practice his reaction and how to control his emotions; maybe rent a bunch of sad movies a few days before his key ceremony and practice not crying at the sad parts. Of course, that might not work because these were happy tears. So what was he supposed to do? Rent a bunch of sappy, happy ending movies and try not to cry? Geez. The whole thing made his eyes water just thinking about it.

The day of the groundbreaking it poured. Not your ordinary, run-of-the-mill rain showers but blinding rain that worked its way beneath every article of clothing you wore. Tower stood shivering and soaked to the bone at the site of where his house would one day be. No one else was there. He swallowed his disappointment and a mouthful of rain and began the long slog home. He supposed he shouldn't be surprised, but he was secretly hoping that the bulldozer guys would have been too manly to have been scared away by a little rain.

All weekend long Tower stared out the windows at the unrelenting rain. His parents were off somewhere and had left him in charge. His sister tried to interest him in a game but Tower's heart wasn't into it. Besides, playing a game with Teeny and all her made up rules required a truckload of patience that Tower just didn't have. He decided to keep his promise of making her some popcorn and the two of them spent Sunday afternoon biting the popcorn into perfect little balls.

The ground clearing finally happened later that week while Tower was at school. He was disappointed he missed it but excited to finally get one step closer to having a house.

CHAPTER TWENTY-ONE

The early part of the building process seemed to take forever. They ran into one delay after another mostly due to weather. Rosemary tried to keep Tower's spirits up by explaining that it was always like this with houses that got started in the winter. He understood in the part of his brain that could analyze things but the emotional side of his brain remained frustrated and impatient.

Then suddenly spring arrived and stuck around. One day Tower and Sky were bundled in coats and the next they were riding home from school in t-shirts, sweatshirts shoved in their backpacks.

"Don't suppose you want to play?" Sky asked. He held his breath hoping for the answer he wanted to hear.

"Can't. I'm working on the house then having dinner at Rosemary's to go over some plans," Tower replied.

He was still as determined as ever to get the house although he was beginning to think his family was actually becoming more normal already. For instance, last week his mother had bought a new blouse for parent-teacher conference. A new blouse, not just new to her from a secondhand store. Tower was amazed. And while his father didn't cut his ponytail he hadn't said "ain't" once in front of the teacher. Tower figured the house would give them even more incentive to be like normal people.

"We never hang out any more. And I'll never see you when you move so far away." Sky was depressed.

"I won't be that far off. And think how cool it will be. No more ratty trailer." He was lost in thought. "A real bedroom. Then I'll be like everybody else."

"Except me. I'll still be in my ratty trailer. You won't want to hang out with the weird kid," Sky said.

"Sure I will. You can come to my house any time you want." Tower reassured Sky.

Sky didn't respond and the boys rode the rest of the way home in silence.

The days passed in a blur of activity for Tower. He was at the new house more often than he was at the trailer. He had a rotating list of places he told his parents he was going, and surprisingly enough, no one questioned it. In fact, his parents seemed preoccupied with something too. Tower thought his father had some big job that his mother was helping him with. She did that sometimes.

✳ ✳ ✳

Trivia sat cross-legged on a small rug outside the trailer and glued unusual found-objects to the frame of a large mirror. She rummaged through a box and selected a rusty hinge and glued it to the frame. Next she picked an old spoon, bent it in a U-shape and glued that on, also. She was focused on her work and was startled when Tower rushed by. "Uh, Tower. I didn't expect you so early."

"Forgot my library card. I've got a big report coming up," he said and ran into the trailer. Trivia watched him go and looked

at her mirror project. She shrugged her shoulders and continued with her art. A few minutes later, Tower hurried past with
his backpack on. He waved.

He sped past his father and Nelson who had an old plank
set up on some sawhorses. His father waved then went back
to measuring the plank and running it through the table saw.
Nelson took the cut boards and began sanding them. He ran his
hand over them to check for splinters.

"These will make a beautiful floor. Things are surely coming
along," Nelson commented.

"Yeah. The plumbing sure gave me nightmares, though." Bo
replied.

By May, the crew was installing the kitchen and the bathroom.
Tower was surprised to discover how much math you used
when you were building a house. It sure made him pay attention in class, now that he knew they were teaching him information that he was truly going to need. Tower eyed the tile saw
and sighed. He wished he could get his hands on it. But the
safety rules forbid it. It seemed no one wanted to risk sending
a twelve-year-old kid to the emergency room with a few less
fingers than he had at the start of the day. Tower understood
but he still wished he could use the wet saw. There was just
something about power tools.

Tower sat in the bathtub and spread the adhesive on the wall
surrounding the tub, then stuck his tiles up and placed spacers
between them to keep everything even. He had picked basic
white tiles with a few random green and blue ones thrown in for
contrast. That meant he didn't have to concentrate on creating a
specific pattern. He didn't think he had the skills for something
too intricate yet.

He wished Sky would have come today, but he had said he was busy with something. It seemed like he was busy a lot lately. Tower was ready to be done with the house. He was tired of spending all his free time working. He wanted to play in the woods and catch frogs and lay in the grass and stare at the clouds. What was the matter with him? Why did he always need something that he didn't have in order to be happy? He shook his head. Maybe he was just tired.

At the end of the day, Tower waved goodbye to Rosemary and trudged home.

When he arrived, he collapsed exhausted onto the couch. His mother was packing a picnic basket and Tower groaned. It couldn't be their Wanda night already, could it?

"There. Now make sure you sit with Wanda while she eats," Trivia said. Tower looked up but she was talking to Teeny.

"She won't eat me, will she?" Teeny's little voice quavered.

"Of course not."

For a split second, Tower was relieved. Then guilt got the better of him. Teeny was barely nine, and even though it wasn't that dark yet due to daylight savings time, Tower was still the big brother. He forced himself to his feet and picked up the basket.

"I'll take it. Although, I'll never understand why she doesn't come here."

Trivia took the basket away, flustered. "You know how bad her arthritis is getting. No, Teeny is getting older and you do so much already." She turned away from Tower and handed Teeny a jacket that resembled Little Red Riding Hood's. Teeny jumped away like she had been burned.

"I'll wear my white sweater," she declared.

"I'll go with you," Tower said but again his mother stopped him.

"No. This will be good for her."

What was going on? Even when Tower whined he still didn't get out of doing a job he didn't want to do. But here he was offering to deliver Wanda's dinner and his mother wouldn't let him. Crazy. He wondered if he was ever going to understand his parents.

"But Wanda's house is way back in the woods," Tower protested.

Trivia guided Teeny out the door. "I'll walk with her. You go rest."

Tower didn't get it but he sank back on the couch, thankfully. He closed his eyes. He was glad that the house was nearing completion. He thought back to when he had first started. Then, he wasn't just tired; he hurt. Muscles all over his body screamed in protest at the over use. Funny. Those muscles rarely hurt now. Tower was impressed with how strong he had become.

CHAPTER TWENTY-TWO

Tower knocked on Rosemary's door.

"Hi." Rosemary opened the door wider to let Tower in.

"Are you busy?"

"Never too busy to share a cup of cocoa with a friend," she replied. Tower smiled. It made him feel good that she referred to him as a friend. She had a way of not treating him like a kid.

She disappeared into the kitchen for a few minutes then returned and handed him a cup.

"Thanks." Tower took a sip. Perfect. Chocolatey and sweet without being gaggingly syrupy.

"It's hard to believe we're down to the finish work, huh?" Rosemary asked.

"I'm beginning to wonder if I made the right choices on the paint and carpet," he said. He tried to visualize what they would look like. He'd had a terrible time deciding in the first place as he had chosen a bunch of swatches that were all very similar colors of tan. The more Tower had looked at them the more they started to blur in his mind. He finally ended up doing eeny-meeny, miney-mo, but now was afraid he had chosen wrong.

Rosemary sat down next to him and considered the choices. "Your mother did help, too, didn't she? I would think she would have liked to choose the colors for her own house."

Rosemary was right. His mother would have loved to choose paint colors if she had known about the house. But then they would have ended up with purple walls with orange peace signs painted on them and that was not going to happen. Not in this house that he had worked so hard on.

"Uh. I helped narrow things down a little for her. You know…" He purposely didn't finish the sentence and let Rosemary draw her own conclusion.

"It can be overwhelming with too many choices," she agreed. "You have a dark tan for the carpet, with a contrasting lighter color for the walls. I think you did fine, Tower."

Tower waffled about his decision. "You don't think that carpet color I picked was too dark?" He was glad the kids at school weren't eavesdropping on this conversation, or he would be in for some more relentless teasing. They would talk to him in a high-pitched voice and say things like "fabulous" when they were talking to him. He didn't know why there had to be so many things that kids could tease you over. It was tough.

"No. I think you want to avoid getting a carpet that's too light or it shows dirt too easily. I think the shade you chose will look fabulous." Tower jerked upright and stared at her suspiciously. She couldn't read minds, could she? That was downright creepy.

"Yeah. Me too. Fabulous." He tried to guess what she was thinking.

"So. It's settled. There's supposed to be a meteor shower tonight. Want to watch?"

"Sure." He tucked the paint swatches into his backpack and followed Rosemary out to the garage. They got a ladder and wrestled it against the house then went back for two sleeping bags.

It was hard climbing the ladder with his hands full of a sleeping bag. "This better be worth it," he said as he shoved the sleeping bag onto the roof ahead of him and climbed after it.

"Anything that'll get you outside on a roof is worth it," Rosemary replied right behind him.

Tower looked at her in surprise. "Grownups like being on roofs?"

"Duh," Rosemary said.

"Duh?" Tower questioned.

"Yeah, duh." They both laughed.

"Who do you think invented them? Kids? I rest my case," Rosemary said.

They spread the sleeping bags on the roof and lay down, eyes gazing skyward. It was peaceful being up there. A slight breeze brushed across their faces but the roof had retained some of the day's heat so they weren't cold.

"I don't see anything," Tower complained.

"You've got to be patient," Rosemary replied.

"I'm not very good at that."

"It's an acquired skill. It comes gradually. Look." She pointed.

Tower moved his head back and forth, frustrated. "I missed it. Which way should I look?"

"You try to focus on one area, you miss the big picture. Just like life. Open your eyes and keep them moving but keep your head still."

Right as she said that there were a series of streaks in the night sky. First one then another, and another. Tower was awestruck.

"Wow. That was cool. You know... I've been thinking a lot about life..." he drifted off, not sure exactly how to explain.

"Yeah?" Rosemary waited for him to go on.

"Tower? Are you up there?" Tower froze at the sound of his father's voice. What on earth was he doing here? And how on earth did he find him? He sat up and turned to Rosemary.

"Uh. I've got to go."

"Who is that?" Rosemary sat up, too.

"My, uh, my Uncle Bo," Tower lied.

"Yo, Bo. Come on up," Rosemary hollered the invitation.

Oh boy. This was bad. This was really bad.

"No. I've got to go. My mom must need me."

He hurried to the ladder to prevent his father from climbing up but he was dreadfully, miserably too late. His father's face appeared at the top of the ladder.

"You must be Rosemary. Sky told me where I could find you Tower."

"Uh, huh." If Tower survived the next few minutes he was going to kill Sky. How could his best friend do this to him?

"See ya later, Rosemary. Thanks for showing me the meteors." Tower tried to edge his father back down the ladder but Bo wasn't budging.

Bo carefully scooted Tower further onto the roof, then climbed up also.

"I love meteor showers," Bo said.

"Yeah. They're great. Come on, have a look. When you're laying down that way, they're mostly coming from the right," she directed Bo.

Tower couldn't believe it when his father lay down on the sleeping bag Tower had vacated. He had no idea what to do now. He hovered next to the ladder anxiously, willing his father to not say a thing.

"So, Bo..." Rosemary began.

"See any yet? They must be all done. We better go," Tower interrupted. He made a big show of clattering the ladder but neither of the adults paid any attention. Bo watched the sky intently. Frustrated, Tower went over and pulled at his father shirtsleeve.

"We should be going," Tower urged.

"Oh. Now you're in a hurry to go home. Seems like…" Tower couldn't chance letting his father finish his sentence.

"I forgot I had homework," Tower said.

That got Bo to his feet. He gave Rosemary an apologetic little smile and gestured to the sleeping bags.

"Do you want some help carrying those down? It seems my boy's got some homework waiting."

With those words Tower's two worlds collided with a crash that had to have been heard in China. It was all over. Everything he had worked for, every nail he had driven in, every muscle he had strained, was all for nothing. He couldn't believe it.

"Mmm. Tower? I don't think we've been properly introduced," Rosemary said calmly.

"That's my dad, Bo," Tower mumbled, as he started down the ladder. "I'm sorry I lied." He backed down the ladder as fast as he could without falling. Although maybe a good coma would keep him from all the explaining he knew he was facing. Or amnesia. No one expected answers from you if you had amnesia.

"What lie? What's he talking about?" Bo was confused and he started after Tower. Rosemary put her hand out to stop Bo. "We need to talk," she said.

Tower skipped the last few rungs of the ladder and leaped to the ground. He ran for home unable to face either of the adults watching him from the roof.

Bo helped Rosemary with the sleeping bags and they climbed down the ladder and went into her house.

Rosemary fixed a couple of cups of cocoa and they sat at the table. They talked for quite awhile then Bo finally got to his feet to leave. He gave Rosemary a smile.

"Thanks for the cocoa. So, we're on the same page?" He took his cup to the sink and washed it.

"Absolutely," she replied.

CHAPTER TWENTY-THREE

Tower went straight to his room and waited anxiously for his father to come home. He didn't know what kind of trouble he would be in, as he had never done anything of this magnitude before. His stomach felt the way it did after he had been on a merry-go-round. Nauseated and going round and round. He couldn't sit still, but there was no room to pace in his little room. After awhile, his mother tapped on his door and told him to get ready for bed.

Tower shut the light off and got into bed. He tried to rehearse his explanation in his mind so he would be ready. There had to be something he could say that would salvage this. He couldn't bear it if he lost this house he had worked so many months on. His thoughts spun in circles until he was dizzy. Somewhere in the middle of his crazy thought process he dropped off to sleep. He never did hear his father return.

In the morning, Tower waited in his room as long as possible before dashing out to the kitchen for breakfast and looked around. His mother and Teeny were going about their day like usual. There was no sign of his father. Weird. No lecture? No note telling him to weed the back garden with a pair of tweezers? He should feel relieved but this living in a state of suspension was worse than an actual punishment. Tower dragged himself out the door; he felt like he hadn't slept at all.

Sky saw Tower coming down the driveway and opened his mouth to explain.

"I had to tell him, Tower. He thought we were together and he said he was worried about you, and you know your dad. He gives you this look that makes you want to come clean. He should have been a priest or a judge." Sky hung his head in shame.

Tower knew exactly what Sky must have felt when his father questioned him. It's not like you were scared of him, more like you didn't want him to look at you with that solemn, "I'm disappointed in you," look that he had. When he gave you that look, you would say anything to make it go away and redeem yourself. He sighed.

"I'm not mad at you. I don't know what I am. Rosemary's going to tell on me and I'll lose the house. My dad is going to give me that look and a list of chores that will take me till my next birthday to finish. I'm doomed." It seemed like such an effort to walk with the weight of the world on his shoulders.

"Things will work out, you'll see."

"Sure," Tower said. Everyone always said things will work out when you faced a problem. What they meant was you'll get used to it; adapt. It didn't mean you'd get what you wanted.

"How were you going to swing that key ceremony thing? And all the paper signing thing?" Sky asked.

"I don't know. I would have come up with a plan."

"Oh yeah. Your plans are great," Sky said.

Tower punched him lightly. "Shut up. You will come to the house with me today, won't you? I could use a friend."

"I can come for a little while, then I have something to do," Sky replied.

After school Tower and Sky headed over to the new house. Tower had spent an anxious day at school, not knowing what was in store for him at the house. He hoped that Rosemary wouldn't have reported him until she'd had a chance to talk to him and get his side. Maybe Tower could convince her how much he needed this house and promise to work on other houses even after he moved into his home.

Tower stood on the front porch and took a deep breath. Sky gave him a thumb's up sign, and they went in. Tower took a close look at the house. He didn't know why he was freaking out over paint colors last night. The place looked great. Tower wandered the house and found Rosemary hanging a door in a back bedroom—the one Tower thought of as Teeny's. She eyed him a second, then asked him to put the pegs through the hinges while she held the door steady. Sky decided to leave the two of them to work this out on their own and went off to work in another part of the house.

Tower crouched down and tapped the first one in. "So...is it okay that I'm here?"

"I don't know Tower, is it?"

Boy, that wasn't a good sign. Tower gulped nervously as he placed the second peg.

"I mean, you didn't tell?"

"Listen, we have a whole bunch of these doors to get to today," Rosemary said.

Tower wanted to scream. Did she tell, or didn't she? "Yeah." Tower paused and tried fishing again. "My dad came in awfully late last night."

"An interesting man, your dad." They went to the next room and started on that door.

"I guess. So...what..." Tower started but was interrupted.

"Listen. I'm not much in a mood to talk."

"Sorry. You're mad, aren't you?"

Rosemary stopped working. "I am kind of mad, Tower. But we have a lot of work to do. So let's get busy."

Tower didn't know what else to say. Obviously she wasn't going to answer his direct questions. And what was worse, she had the same disappointed way of looking at you as his father did. Tower decided to throw all of his energy into the work and hope that it would be enough to get back into her good graces.

He finished hanging all the interior doors, then assisted with hanging all the light fixtures. His arms ached from holding lights over his head while they were being wired and connected to the ceiling. He helped mount the shelves and closet rods in all the closets. Finally, he was so exhausted he collapsed against a wall to take a break. He had hardly made it to the floor, when Rosemary walked by.

"Up, boy. We're not done yet."

"It's nine o'clock. I'm tired," Tower complained.

Rosemary pointed over at a woman and her two young children who were washing windows. The kids couldn't have been more than nine or ten.

"Quit your boo-hooing. You're not the only one who wants a house. We need to finish yours, so we can start on theirs."

Tower looked at the little family for a few seconds, then took a deep breath and struggled to his feet. Rosemary was being so unfair. He had worked since four that afternoon and all he had had for dinner was a bag of trail mix left over from lunch. He got some cleaning supplies and began scrubbing the bathroom. Finally, he could not move another muscle, lift another scrub brush, or probably even make it to the front door to go home. Everyone but him and Rosemary had left long ago.

The house gleamed. Tower felt a glow of pride and a whole host of other emotions warring inside him as he took a last look at the house before heading home. He didn't hear Rosemary come up behind him.

"Here," she said and handed him a brand new, shiny key. "Saturday you'll get the ceremonial key, but this is the one that will open the door." She walked off before Tower could say a word.

Tower turned the key over and over in his hand. His plan of redeeming himself by working himself to the bone must have worked. He looked at the key. Funny. He would have expected to feel more emotion, but he was numb. He squeezed his hand over the key, closed his eyes and waited for the feeling of happiness and anticipation to wash over him, but it did not happen. What did happen was he got all wobbly from fatigue and having his eyes shut and almost toppled over. He shoved the key in his pocket and trudged home.

It seemed impossible that his body could be this tired and still move. It was like he was on automatic pilot. He needed a good night's sleep, or maybe a dozen then maybe he would feel back to normal. Or should he say back to usual?

By some miracle, he managed to make it home. He dragged past his mother who was on the verge of nodding off on the couch. "Night, Mom," he said, without breaking stride. Trivia blinked her eyes groggily.

Tower entered his room and fell onto the bed. He was asleep before he could get his shoes off.

Trivia had about drifted off again when Bo clomped in the front door, pulled off his boots and let them land on the floor with a thud. He collapsed on the couch next to her and groaned.

"What is it they say? What doesn't kill you just makes you wish it did?" Bo asked.

Trivia smiled. "Makes you stronger."

"I like my version better. Come on woman if I sit here any longer, I may never get up." They lurched to their feet.

"Are you sure we're doing the right thing? Tower looked exhausted," she said with motherly concern.

"I'm sure. What is it they say...?"

CHAPTER TWENTY-FOUR

Tower was still worn out by the time he returned home from school. All he wanted to do was crawl into bed and burrow deep under his covers. He tossed his backpack into a corner of the living room and headed to his room, but his mother blocked him.

"I need you to do something today," she said.

"I'm beat, Mom. Can't it wait?"

Trivia shook her head. "Sorry, buddy. I need you to take Teeny around the neighborhood to sell her magazine subscriptions."

Teeny bounced up and down. "I want to win. I want to win."

"Mom, I can't," Tower said.

"There is no can't Tower. There's only won't, and believe me, in this case won't is not an option. March. Stay close to your sister."

Tower stomped outside angrily. He was so mad he didn't even hold the door open for Teeny. Teeny, pigtails tied with bright ribbons, skipped her little legs as fast as she could so she could catch up.

"Now be real cute at the first couple of houses so we can get some sales and go home," he coached her.

"Nope. We're out here until my feet won't skip. I'm going to win," Teeny said.

"It's just some stupid prize," Tower said.

Teeny stopped skipping and gave Tower a hurt look.

"Do you think the school would give me a stupid prize, even if I was the best seller ever?"

Tower felt bad when he saw how disappointed she was. "Nah. I'm just being a grouch. I bet the prizes are awesome. Come on, let's go sell some magazines."

That cheered Teeny back to her usual bubbly self and she bounded up the sidewalk to a house. Tower waited on the sidewalk. His mother told him to stay close; she didn't say stay connected. Besides, he could see Teeny fine from here.

He hoped this didn't take all afternoon. He wasn't expected at the house today but he was still physically and emotionally drained from the last two days.

It must have been the pigtails or the ribbons but Teeny was good at selling. Tower was terrible at it. He didn't know if it was because he was embarrassed going door to door, or if he didn't believe in the products he had been given to sell in the past, or maybe he wasn't as sweet as Teeny was. Whatever it was she was clearly the salesman in the family and possibly, judging by her order form, the school.

They arrived at a house that looked familiar to Tower. It had a For Sale sign in the yard, and a woman was planting flowers along the front walk. All of a sudden, it occurred to Tower why he knew this house. It looked different in the daylight, and he didn't remember a For Sale sign, but there was no doubt in Tower's mind that this was Jeremy's house. Before he could stop her Teeny made a beeline for the woman.

"No, Teeny. Not this house." But it was too late. She was halfway up the walk. Tower's stomach knotted up. He hadn't had any actual run-ins with Jeremy since that day on the school steps that bought Jeremy a three day suspension but Tower had seen the ugly looks Jeremy threw his way every chance he got, and he didn't want to push his luck.

"Well, hello. I see you're selling this beeeautiful house and probably don't want magazine subscriptions for yourself, but do you know they make wonderful gifts?" Teeny asked in her best salesperson voice.

"Huh?" the woman replied.

"Yes. My name is Christina Marigold Adam and I am selling magazine subscriptions for my school." She held out her catalog.

"Teeny, don't bother this lady. She's obviously busy." Tower tried desperately to persuade his sister but Teeny was in full-blown glory in her role as magazine sales child.

"We even have some of those fancy magazines that dentist's offices have. The ones with the sparkly Chand-A-Leers." Jeremy's mother looked tempted. Tower couldn't believe it. So this is how Teeny did it. She didn't take no personally, and she kept hammering away at people till she found their weak spot.

Jeremy's mother took off her gardening gloves and took the catalog. "I suppose I could take a look."

"Mahvellous. Now if I could trouble you for the use of a water closet facility, I would be ever most grateful." Teeny smiled sweetly.

"Teeny," Tower warned.

"You know how to push your luck, don't you? All right, go on," Jeremy's mother said, not at all graciously.

Teeny grabbed Tower's hand but he refused to budge. "I'll wait here."

Jeremy's mother looked up from the catalog. "Go with her. I don't want her making a mess."

Tower looked at Teeny's feet. It's not like she had stepped in mud or dog doo, or something. And she was nine, not two. She knew how to go to the bathroom by herself, for crying out loud. But once again, he was overruled. That seemed to be the theme for today. What is it Tower wanted to do? Too bad; overruled. He reluctantly walked with Teeny up to the front door.

"You owe me big time," he said.

Teeny rang the bell. Tower started to feel queasy. Jeremy answered the door and an ugly little smile crossed his face. How could a smile, which should look happy, look so evil?

"Well if it ain't Mr. Teacher's Pet, Coat Drive, Hippie Boy." Jeremy sized Tower up.

"Excuse me, but the flower planting lady said I could use your bathroom," Teeny said.

Jeremy peered out at his mother who nodded her head. He opened the door grudgingly, and Tower and Teeny went inside.

The entryway floor was made of hardwood, and polished and buffed to a high glow. Teeny eyed the floor a second, then slipped off her shoes. Tower looked at Jeremy who wasn't wearing shoes. Thinking it better not to rock the boat, Tower also stepped out of his shoes.

Jeremy led Teeny past a living room furnished in all white and glass and pointed to a door. "It's in there. Don't use the fancy towels. They're props."

Teeny tipped her head graciously and shut the door behind her.

Tower felt squirmy and uncomfortable. How did he end up here? First they dumpster-dived from Jeremy's house and now his sister happened to pick this particular house to have to use the bathroom. What were the odds? How could he have such bad luck? It was a good thing Tower was too young to gamble because he would lose his shirt.

Tower looked around the living room while he waited for Teeny. It was impressive. There wasn't a speck of dust anywhere on the glass tables, and the silver pillows on the couch looked like no one's head or back had ever come into contact with them. The room was decorated with enormous vases that held a bunch of weird looking sticks. Nothing in it made Tower feel comfortable.

"Uh, this is a nice room. Bet you all have some fun times in here." Tower tried to make conversation.

Jeremy snorted. "In here? Are you making fun of me? Up in my room, I've got all kinds of cool stuff. I've got an Xbox 360 and Nintendo and a plasma television," he said.

Tower wasn't exactly sure what any of those things were. Least of all a plasma television. Wasn't plasma something in your blood? He looked around.

"But where does your family hang out?"

"I guess in their rooms. This is a big house. We've got lots of rooms," Jeremy said.

Tower didn't understand. "Everyone goes somewhere separate? Like all the time?"

Jeremy was getting mad. "Listen, hippie boy. We're not all touchy-feely like you guys, okay? We don't sit around and sing Kumbaya. We need our space."

The last thing Tower wanted to do was to get Jeremy mad. "Sorry."

Apparently that was the wrong thing to say, and here he thought he was trying to keep the peace, but Jeremy's face flushed and he clenched his fists.

"No. No way. You are not feeling sorry for me."

Tower began to get a little scared. Surely Jeremy wouldn't haul off and hit him in his own house, would he? With his mother right outside? Tower wouldn't put anything past Jeremy, though. He wanted to get out of here. Now. What on earth was Teeny doing in the bathroom?

What she was doing was enjoying her encounter with a bathroom straight out of one of her fairy tales. The wallpaper had a fuzzy gold pattern and Teeny ran her fingers over it. The mirror was huge and heavy looking with an intricate frame with cherubs at the corners. She did a little pirouette and admired her image. Then she washed her hands; with water only because she didn't want to spoil the fancy clam-shaped soaps. She looked at the fancy towels, tied with tassel-tipped gold ropes, that the growly boy had told her not to use. She didn't see any other towels so she rubbed her hands carefully on the underside of the towel where nobody would notice.

Teeny finally emerged from the bathroom and Tower urged her to the front door. He couldn't get out of this house fast enough.

Outside, Jeremy's mother handed Teeny back the catalog and shook her head.

"I don't know what I was thinking. I can't go spending money on a stinking magazine. She sighed with remorse. "Just last week I had a gardener."

Teeny took her catalog back and held her head high. "Just last week I had a cold." She turned and flounced away. Tower rushed after her, glad to breathe some fresh air. Teeny turned hurt eyes Tower's way. "Tower, my magazines don't stink. In fact, some of them have little perfumes inside."

There was the sound of running feet behind them. Tower turned and watched, horrified, as Jeremy reached out and grabbed Teeny's shoulder roughly and spun her around.

"I told you not to use the towels!" Jeremy said. He shook Teeny like a rag doll.

Tower reacted with a gut instinct to protect his sister. He didn't stop to think, he didn't stop to reason it out, he simply hauled off and threw a whale of a punch right to Jeremy's jaw. Jeremy flew to the ground and landed with the force of a bag of concrete dropped from a twelve-foot balcony. He moaned and held his face.

Tower bent down to check on his sister.

"Are you okay?" he asked.

She nodded, eyes wide.

"I'm glad." Tower reached out for Teeny's hand. "Your magazines are not what's wrong with that family."

They turned and left Jeremy still rolling around on the sidewalk.

CHAPTER TWENTY-FIVE

ower and Sky trotted down the steps in front of the school. A few of the classmates waved at them.

"See ya tomorrow guys," one girl said. Tower and Sky waved back at her. Tower marveled at how much had changed at school since the blanket drive. People treated him like one of the gang. Like normal? Tower thought so but he was beginning to wonder what normal even was. Was it only having two of things so the things don't start to own you? Or not wanting your food to touch? Was it using a plastic Popeye bubble pipe to quit smoking? Was it living in a huge house where everybody had their own spaces and never spent any time together? Or was it living in a commune with a family that ate dinner together, and had family nights, and a little Velcro window that would open right when you needed a little comfort?

He had done a lot of thinking since he socked Jeremy. He didn't feel guilty that he had resorted to physical violence but he didn't feel proud either. He had discovered that most of the time his father was right; you could walk away from an actual fight. But there were also times when a big brother had to protect a little sister, especially from a bully kid three times her size.

Tower took the key to his new house out of his pocket and squeezed it tight until the ridges dug into his palm. He kicked at a few clumps of dirt, turning something over in his head. He finally took a deep breath and straightened his shoulders.

"Sky? Rosemary gave me the key to the house the other day."

Sky seemed distracted and in a hurry. "Yeah. That's great. I told you it would work out."

Tower nodded solemnly. Sky was right. Things did work out all right, even if it wasn't exactly the way you had originally planned.

"I'm supposed to meet Rosemary for dinner tonight. Maybe she wants to talk or something, but first I've got something to do. I can't walk home with you today. Sorry," Tower said.

Sky ducked his head so Tower wouldn't see the relief in his eyes. "No problem. See you."

Tower waited till Sky was out of sight before walking across the street to Vic's DeliMart. It had one of the few pay phones still left in town. The phone company's assumption that everyone had cell phones was one of Tower's pet peeves. He tried awkwardly to balance the phone book on one thigh while he looked up a number. The metal cable that attached the book to the booth was way too short and it was nearly impossible to use. That was another thing that annoyed Tower. Old-fashioned phone booths were a design marvel. You had shelter from the elements, privacy and a little shelf to place the phone book. These current little egg-shaped structures provided none of that.

Finally Tower had conquered the phone book, found the number, made a call and settled in to wait for his cab. He checked and double checked his money and hoped he had enough. He didn't know what they did to you if you came up short. Make you wash and wax the car?

In the cab, Tower watched the meter thingy closely. It had a metronome like quality to its clicking, and if he weren't so nervous he might have actually fallen asleep. The cab pulled to a stop and Tower paid the driver and got out.

Tower steadied his nerves and entered the building. He looked around for a receptionist or a sign that would tell him where to go. He loved those, "you are here" signs that you found at shopping malls and other large buildings, but he always had to picture them as if they were laying flat on the floor before he could orient himself to which way he was facing and which way he needed to go.

It took him awhile but he found the office he was looking for and walked up to the young receptionist behind the desk.

"I need to see the director of the Neighbor For Neighbor program," he said.

"Do you have an appointment?" she asked. Right, like he had planned this in advance. Besides, who gave appointments to twelve-year-old kids?

He shook his head. "It's important."

She dialed a number. "There's a young man here to see you. He says it's important. He says his name is..." She looked questioningly at Tower.

"Tower Adam," he stated.

"Tower Adam," she repeated into the phone. "Right. Bye." The receptionist hung up the phone and turned to Tower. "She said you could wait in her office. She'll be there in a minute."

The receptionist escorted Tower to an inner office.

It was a large room comfortably but simply furnished with a desk and walls lined with bookshelves. The bookshelves held books. Lots and lots of books. There were no silly little figurines or other dust gathering items on the shelves. Tower headed over to a chair placed in front of the desk, but he was too restless to sit. He picked up a photo, one of a few items out on the desk.

"That's her family. A tragedy," the receptionist said.

Tower looked at the picture of a young man and a small boy examining a seashell on the beach. "What happened?" he asked.

"They died in a car accident. It was years ago."

Tower put the photo back on the desk quickly. "Oh."

"After it happened, she gave up her law practice and started the Neighbor For Neighbor program," the receptionist continued.

"That will be all, Cynthia."

The receptionist blushed and left the room quickly, clearly embarrassed that the director had caught her discussing her private life.

Tower stood rooted to the floor, stunned, and stared at the director of the Neighbor For Neighbor house building organization.

"I didn't think I was going to see you till dinner," Rosemary said.

"You're the director here?" Tower was having a hard time making his brain work.

"Yes."

"So even though you knew I was a liar, you let me keep the house?" This was unreal.

"I figured you had your reasons if you were willing to go to so much trouble."

Tower paced back and forth. He tried to think of the right words to explain it all to her. It was important to him that she understood.

"I thought having a house would make me normal. Us a normal family." He looked up at her. He sighed and plunked down the key he had been clutching in his hand all afternoon. "I want the next family on the list to have my house."

As soon as he said that Tower felt a sense that all was right with his world.

"Are you sure?" Rosemary asked.

Tower nodded. "We're weird. Living in a house wouldn't change that. But, you know, there's good weird and there's bad weird." He shrugged. "We're good weird."

"Yeah, you are. You spend time together. Your parents didn't need to lose someone to realize how important that is." Rosemary's eyes strayed to the photo on her desk.

"Is that why you live in the little house with hardly any stuff?" Tower was beginning to understand.

"You know that bumper sticker, 'he who dies with the most toys' wins?" she asked.

"Yeah."

"It's crap. It isn't things that make you happy. I worked a lot so my family could have nice things, and then once they had died, all I had was this big house filled with things; things that I had to dust and polish. And nowhere near enough memories because I got home too late to even tuck my son in. I have lots of memories of peeking in at him sleeping, but where are the memories of watching him discovering a roly-poly bug, or eating a chocolate cupcake, or learning how to ride a two wheel bike?"

Tower thought about this. Rosemary was right. Oh, things might make you happy for a little while, but then the good feelings faded and before too long you found yourself wanting something else to try to make yourself happy. Happy had to come from somewhere else. Like old friends who stood by you even when you came up with stupid schemes. And new friends who saw through your lies and liked you anyway.

Rosemary looked at her watch. "So, are you ready for that dinner?"

CHAPTER
TWENTY-SIX

Rosemary and Tower's dinner was supposed to be a celebration over the completion of the house. And that is exactly what it was. It didn't matter that it wasn't going to be Tower's house. In a way, he was more excited today knowing that it was going to that mother and two children, than he was when he thought it was going to be his family's. He would never have believed it possible.

Tower took one last bite and pushed his plate away.

Rosemary glanced at her watch, then excused herself from the table to make a phone call. Tower saw her nod her head before she hung up and returned to the table.

"We should get going," he said.

"In a minute. I sure could use a hot cup of coffee." Rosemary sat down and signaled the waitress.

"It's getting late. My folks will be worried."

Rosemary laughed. "Tower, you've been late nearly every night in the last couple of months. What's your hurry?"

The waitress came and Rosemary ordered a cup of coffee and two pieces of pie.

"I kind of need to talk to my father. I haven't seen him since that night on your roof. I could be in all kinds of trouble." He, all of a sudden, needed to make things right with his father. He didn't want to sit here and eat a piece of pie. But there was no way to get out of it without being rude to Rosemary, and how could he do that after all she had done for him?

When the pie came, Tower gobbled it as fast as he could and looked up at Rosemary expectantly when he was done. He had to force himself from groaning out loud when he saw her plate. Her piece was barely touched, and she still had an almost full cup of coffee. She blew on it and took a tiny sip.

"I love this restaurant, don't you?" Rosemary asked.

Great. Now she was going to make small talk. How could he get her to hurry up and eat? Whoa. There he went again trying to will someone to do something. When was he going to learn? He could barely control his own actions, how did he expect to control everybody else's? There was plenty of time to make things right with his father. He needed to be patient. He smiled at Rosemary.

"Yeah. It's great. Thanks for dinner."

After what seemed like an eternity, Rosemary was ready to leave. She excused herself to use the restroom and Tower felt his newfound patience start to melt away. Breathe, he told himself.

On the drive home Tower was quiet. He reflected on all that had happened in the last few days. What a whirlwind. He was at the point now where he had a sense of peace, which he hoped would endure once he had squared things with his father.

He was deep in these thoughts as Rosemary pulled to a stop outside his family's trailer. Tower looked around in confusion. He felt like you did when you woke from a dream, where you were disoriented trying to figure out the real from the dream. But he knew this was no dream. Rosemary stood on the other side of the car watching him. There was something seriously off kilter here. Had he landed in Oz? The spot in front of him, where his home had stood for his entire life, was now occupied by what looked like Wanda's trailer.

What was going on?

Luckily he was spared the ordeal of having to solve this dilemma, because next thing he knew his father came over and shook Rosemary's hand.

"Thanks for keeping him occupied," Bo said.

Tower looked at Rosemary accusingly. She smiled back at him sweetly.

"What is going on? Where's our house?" Tower asked.

Bo didn't answer. He put his hand on Tower's shoulder and guided him across the grounds and deep into the woods toward where Wanda's trailer was formerly parked. Tower heard a commotion in front of him, looked up, and was stunned to see the entire community standing there. En masse, they parted and let Bo and Tower through. Trivia, Teeny, Sky and Rosemary followed closely.

Tower opened his mouth but before he could speak, Bo said, "hit it," and a floodlight came on illuminating the Adam's trailer. Above and beyond the trailer, built around an enormous tree, was an intricate treehouse. The crowd cheered and clapped wildly.

A line of tiny white lights wound around newly planted baby trees led up to the huge tree. The treehouse was a thing of pure beauty. There was a weather-beaten barn door that formed one wall, with three portholes cut out of it for windows. On another side was a tiny balcony with a salvaged iron railing.

"What is that?" Tower finally managed to find his voice.

"That's your new house, son. I know how much you wanted one."

"You built this?" Tower couldn't believe it. When did his father have the time? And how on earth was it that Tower hadn't noticed? He remembered how odd his mother acted that last time it was their Wanda dinner night. They must have been in the middle of the construction then. But, obviously, the trailers weren't moved till some time today. Tower shook his head in amazement.

"We all did," Bo replied and gestured to the rest of the commune residents.

Tower looked around at his neighbors. They beamed with pride. He smiled at them, then turned to Rosemary.

"You knew about this?"

"Just since the meteor night. Your dad and I had a little talk." Rosemary and Bo exchanged a smile.

"Don't dawdle, boy. Come on up." Bo urged him.

Tower didn't need a second invitation. He followed Bo to a ladder suspended beneath the treehouse and the two of them climbed up and emerged through a hatch in the floor. Bo entered first and turned on a light. Tower hopped up the last step and scanned his surroundings.

The room was small and odd-shaped, following the contour of the tree. A couch that doubled as a bed stood along the length of one wall. A built-in shelf held a tiny CD player and a reading light that shined down onto the couch.

"There's electricity?"

"Yeah. The place is fully functional. It's all weather proofed and there's even plumbing. I can't believe you didn't notice all the extra gray hairs I've gotten lately," Bo joked.

Tower wandered around the room, touching everything. He recognized the mirror his mother had been working on hanging on the tree trunk. He bent down and stroked the floorboards.

"Nice patina," he said.

He entered a galley-style kitchen with a mosaic tile counter top and salvaged cupboards.

Sky tapped him on the shoulder and pointed to the tan walls. "I picked out the paint color."

Tower had to smile. "Nice. Brown."

"No, it's burnt nutmeg," Sky paused. "This is a lot closer than that other house."

"Yeah. A good place to hang out."

"Yeah."

Tower continued the tour and entered the tiny bathroom. He immediately burst out laughing when he saw the shower. There, as the shower bottom, was the large utility sink that they had reclaimed from Jeremy's garbage. Bo beamed at Tower.

"Came in handy, didn't it?" Bo asked.

Tower shook his head in amazement. "This is soooo...one of a kind."

Bo clapped him on his shoulder. "No one can accuse me of building some run of the mill treehouse."

Tower jumped up on his father and wrapped his whole body around him in a bear hug. "Of course not, because you're weird," he said.

Bo caught him and hugged him back. "And proud of it, too."

Bo set Tower down. Yep, they were weird, and probably always would be. But that was all right. Tower understood that now. They had their own way of doing things.

Teeny cleared her throat a few times to get Tower's attention. Finally he looked over at her. "I got you a present." She held out a package.

"You did?" Tower opened the present and discovered a set of walkie-talkies. He looked at his sister.

"For night time. So we can still talk," Teeny said solemnly.

"Cool." Tower knew that they would put them to good use, talking about houses and flying horses and red squiggly things floating in their eyes and a whole bunch of other things he couldn't even imagine yet. He gave his sister a hug.

Trivia went into the kitchen, and bent down into the dormitory sized refrigerator and got out some ice cream. "Who wants some ice cream?" she asked. She opened the little cupboard and took out two bowls. "Oh, dear. Tower, you're going to need some more bowls."

Tower looked into the cupboard and saw a neat arrangement of two of everything. He looked over at Rosemary who smiled at him then he looked around at everyone else in the room.

"It's okay. I've got everything I need," Tower said.

It was funny how things worked out sometimes. You wished for one thing, and then you got something better than you could have even dreamed of having. Somehow, Tower's father had sensed his need for a new house. Tower thought he needed a regular, every day kind of house but his father knew better. He had enlisted the help of Tower's family and friends and together they had created this treehouse. This nowhere-near-normal treehouse.

THE END